LE PROJET

erret

★

C · P · SERRET

NEVER
HUMAN

TEMPEST & GAYLE⸍
PHŒNIX⸍
MMXXIV.

Published by
Tempest & Gayle
PHOENIX

Design by C. P. Serret

Set in Seria

ISBN: 978-1-7343234-8-1

LCCN 2024908346

for the irresonant void

NEVER HUMAN

Tu ſe ombra, et ombra uedi.
—DANTE, Purgatorio, Canto XXI.

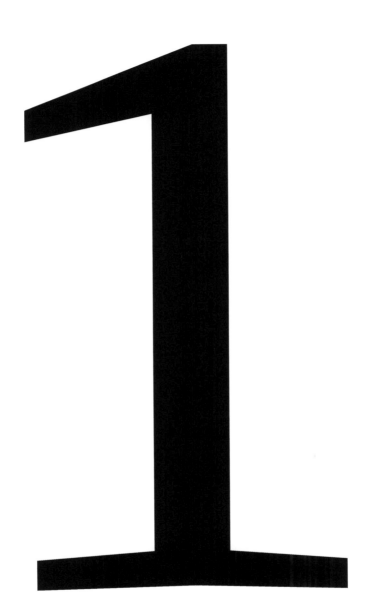

Serret, Never Human,
I.

H   *e learned to swallow his voice.* Hollow things echo. Don't speak.

—*That*, she said.

She was pasty and soft, pointing with a limp, withdrawn hand. Green eyes. No, greenish grey, not looking at him.

Sideways in her seat, her limp hair was dead yellow grass crowned with a rainbow of butterfly clips. There was no mistaking it. The pinched eyebrows, the crinkled nose, and the twisted upper lip of her open mouth.

He was encircled by her clique, caught in his cold blue chair, a shiny woodlike tablet angled above his legs. They were all like that. Columns and rows. Everyone caught.

The room was grey, but it was green and open outside the glass. Grey like the City Of, but that was far away. It smelled green outside, but not in here.

He hadn't listened to what they'd been saying, their awkward lines, like when the TV is on and you aren't watching. They each would say things, and the others would echo them. Or pretended to. Or were supposed to.

—Ismaël, the French Madame called him, est-ce que vous parlez anglais?

—Sí...

The chorus groaned, but Madame talked about the French si in English; then she called on someone else. It was all rote. Like a basic echo command:

French Mme:~> echo «Je parle français!»
Je parle français!

The French Madame was American and taller than the tallest boy in the grey room and had big yellow hair like a star in an old movie. With her squeaking white cursor, she scrawled on the green plane that covered most of the front wall. Command lines.

Dead Grass had turned back around in her seat. Her layered tank bared her shoulders and upper back, giving him a glimpse of the razor edge of her hollow. Her softness was as thin as an eggshell, the visible sliver of emptiness in unlit shadow.

They were all the same under their tees, polos, and button-ups. All hollow.

It was hard not to look, impossible not to see it wink when she squirmed in her seat. No one, not even the smaller ones at the red house, had ever admitted to seeing it, but they knew how to lie, too. He'd learned to play off the «joke»; then he'd stopped joking.

You could feel the invisible surface, the warm skin over sinew and bone. Like a glass egg with a partially painted shell, you can see inside, but you can't stick your finger in. A surface that showed in mirrors, photos, and on TV, through windowpanes or an empty glass. Even Saran Wrap.

His own back, in the mirror, too, showed unbroken skin. There was no way to see, no way to be sure. He only saw hollows directly with his naked eyes.

Most of the time, he didn't think about it. Most of the time, he didn't have to see. But it was hard not to look at that beckoning gap into shadows till one of the others teased, hissing,

—Omigod, he's staring: I think he likes you.

There were muted *ewws* and other mimes of outrage till Madame called on one of them. He listened to everyone say what they were supposed to say, stumbling and faltering on cue.

Words were less than empty. He watched every hollow gesture, every feigned expression. Each was alone in her performance, following her cues, as isolated as his observance. The buzzer ended the routine.

They poured out of the grey room into a grey hallway patched with sections of blue. It looked the same in both directions. Rows of doors, sharp turns right and left, stairwells down and up. A square circuit of rooms, three levels high. They bunched and flowed past each other in a fluid dynamic. More lines. Barking. Hooting. Routines and subroutines.

The carpet was cleaner than the sidewalks in the City Of. He sat by himself against the wall like they did together, on standby for the next thing. You started with a sheet of numbers and times. Each number was a room, the times a sequence of rooms. A program of routines. A loop of the program till they give you a new sheet.

His bookbag was a darker grey, like concrete in the rain. He took out his pad and a yellow pencil, No. 2. It wasn't finished. There was pressure behind each line, an incompressible solidity that travelled down through the fragile graphite tip.

Pale-blue doll eyes, clear and shiny like glass, she looks down at him. Long hair, yellow gold, she wears shades of blue. The blue jeans faded. The blue polo, navy; the little man and horse, red. She says, She's such a bitch.

He shrugs, saying, Nothing new. He didn't want to say anything.

You're Ismael, right? I'm Sophie.

Her features are sharp, the only softness implied by the diffusion of light over her skin. She drops and sits crosslegged beside him; she smells like soap. Green soap. You like to draw?

He shrugs.

Sophie says, What are you drawing? A cowboy?

A robot from an old movie.

Why would a robot dress up like a cowboy?

He doesn't know he's a robot.

How can he not know?

Nobody told him.

Is he even a him?

He thinks so.

Can he really think, or is he just pretending to?

Ismael shrugs again and says, How could you tell the difference?

Sophie watches him draw, then says, You like machines?

All the parts have to fit together. I can understand them.

Even when they don't understand themselves? Is that okay?

Ismael doesn't have an answer to that. Is it worse to know?

She says, Don't you think they're scary?

He says, Scarier than what?

The doors opened. The Art Misses was grey, turning white. The art rooms were white, like the inner surface of the hollows. It was like stepping inside.

A place of flat surfaces and solids. He'd asked the Science Mister about curved surfaces without saying hollow, and he'd said that was mathematics. He asked the Math Mizz, and she talked about advanced placement.

Waiting clusters dispersed to the level-top desks set edge-to-edge in unbroken white rows. All mid and longer-haired, shes: yellow hair, brown, and red, but for him. His was short and, in mirrors, black. He preferred to sit in the middle, in the gaps between their clusters. He'd learned to hide in the crowd.

A new assignment, Art Misses explained. Mixed media. Not the unambigüous surfaces he preferred but one cluttered and obscured.

No pencils, then, or ink, but acrylics, glue, and aluminum foil. Matte side out, the lid of a trash can was seated ajar, as seen from above. A tilted circle. The inside was only a crescent, shiny side out, a fuzzy mirror in oblonged eclipse. A dollop of putty on the sidewalk grid painted black like old bubblegum. Period. Signed, Icy. He had nothing else to say – he'd been nabbed tagging «Icy» and had ended up in the System.

The Art Misses asked if everything was okay: they

had two periods to finish. She suggested an impasto technique to add pavementlike texture. Next time.

Sophie meets him on the stairs, going down. Lunch? she says.

He nods but is still on the trash can: he hasn't thought about them as a shape – another complex surface around a hollow. He'll have to look at one on the way to the red house. There might be more details.

Her green soap is lost in the shuffle of heated breath and stale, mid-day sweat. She says, Is Art your favourite class?

I guess.

Could you draw me? she says, smiling.

I guess, but not for class.

Okay, later.

He split off with some of the shuffling shoes into a wider, dimmer space. Grey pillars rose to the high ceiling. It didn't smell like the lanes outside of restaurants at dinner time. There was the acrid tinge of smoke on steam and a thicker pungence: meaty, metallic, and acid. The feed was twice a day. More than the soup kitchens, but the smell was about the same.

Long lines were nothing new, and compared to back then, he wasn't even hungry. It was spooned out with long satin-silver handles. Covered hair. Smooth steel surfaces, not those crinkle-cornered aluminum trays.

Rows of rectangular brown planes rested on black webs of tubing. Orange ellipses were suspended alongside them. Rigid lines of separation and mushroomlike perches for stranger things than cartoon caterpillars.

They segregated themselves by hair length. He sat, centring himself within an interstice, three empty seats on each side. Shorter-hairs only on this half of the space.

The tray was orange, too. Flat bits of sheet metal, an eggshell plate, three wet blots, yellow, brown, and green.

They complained about their spoonfuls. He'd had

worse, but he knew the emptiness folding in towards
his spine like a twisted balloon.

No matter how much they ate, they were always
empty. You could complain when you weren't hungry
or afraid. They'd never had to search or hide except as a
game.
—Hey!

Puffy, pasty, too, and piglike.
—Hey, where are you from?

Ruddy surfaces, bowl hair. Not a part of his program
either. Ismael said,
—Here?
—Why's this kid so stupid? Where? are? you? from?

They wanted something farther away.
—Belize, said Ismael.
—Where the fuck is that? Mexico?
—Central America.
—So, Mexico. Jeez, this dumbass.

Piggy said,
—Why don't you go back there?
—I can't, said Ismael.
—Why not?
—I was born here.
—So? You can still go back

Ismael shook his head. There was no going back – not
from the trash.
—This dumbass...

The other gaps would be the same, and he could see
that girl from here. April. Long, dark, straight hair. There
was something different about her, though she was the
same: the same gestures, the same lines. She was in part
of his program.

He cleaned his plate, and they started in on him
again, mocking how he'd finished his peas off of the
tipped surface. Are you gonna cry? they said. Gonna cry?

Quitting the routine, «this dumbass», the «that», and
sometimes «it», returned his tray. Outside, a blacktop
grid of chalk lines painted with broad brush strokes.

He'd emerged from the wide rectangular brick surface, a line of «happy trees» opposite. The blacktop was a charcoal rub, uneven shades of grey, the grid, a gameboard of leftover Hot Wheels. There were lots of brick walls in the City Of, lots of grey towers, lots of glass. Lots of Hot Wheels. Every surface was subject to the interplay of shadow and light, even their inner surfaces.

This wall was like one side of a cube sunk into the ground. On the other side was the open green with its fences, but they would be there, too. The liquid plane above was marbled blue and white, an upside-down sea.

It was a middle place, they'd said, before a higher place. The higher place would also be a middle place. A «preparatory» place for the last middle place, before «your future». Unless he chose more middle places. You had to choose your programs in advance, and that, too, was a test. That's what they'd said when they'd picked this program for him this time: trilingual better than bilingual. Next time, it was his test. They were a part of the System.

For a long time, he'd been stuck outside. He'd been cold. He'd been wet. He'd looked into grey buildings, brick buildings like this one, empty at night with their lights on. Their clean, dry carpets. He'd slept on the pavement right next to their locked doors. Slept under overhangs that staved off the rain or the morning dew and in hollows that let the wind blow by. You had to lay something down over concrete's leeching cold, but he'd learned to leave before anyone showed up. To make it like he'd never been. Leave no trace and use it again.

He'd bought a Casio with his lawnmower money. Their Swatchs stepped from second to second, showing the hollow between moments. LCDs covered the gaps behind a digital mask. Covered what was hidden in now. It was time, now, to go back. There was no buzzer outside, but the shadows had changed shape. Some of them had folding radios that showed the time, but the misters and misses would take them if they saw.

Passing from outside to inside, a membrane of tension tried to repel him. The plastic light, grey walls, and the steps of uncounted sacrifices. For the future. He'd heard the tears of children bring rain, but they didn't know that here or didn't say. That was Mexico.

Had he really been Kekchí, too? Had he counted? Sacrificed not to a Well, but thrown to the City Of. He'd lost the names, except for the god of mountains, but there were no mountains near.

Long hairs crowded the front row of the grey space, variations on a theme. Bright shirts, jeans, and shorts. He sat in the second, not behind April, but on the diagonal. Her bare legs were crossed away from him, one bare foot freed of its boat shoe. A contrast of surfaces. Translucent white marble, brown leather – LL Bean, like a lot of them. He was learning.

Her brown hair was centre-parted and curled only against her clothes. It would be hard to paint, streaked with lighter strands. Her eyes, never looking at him... charcoal, Ti white, and a dab of Prussian blue. He could follow the thin arcs of her eyebrows, the uptilt of her nose. The swollen crescents of her lips, smiling not at him. Flesh tint acrylic.

He traced the line of her limb, over the knee and down her instep, to the piano-key fit of her small toes. Pressure surged down to its level. It pulsed, an aching discomfort reaching out to her, tight against his thigh.

What trudged in behind her wasn't the Math Mizz but a Substitute Mister, almost grey in his faded dishevelment. Hunched plaid; chinos; and a dilapidated bag, brown leather. A hollow folded in on itself.
—Shoes on, please.

Ismael flinched from the Substitute Mister, noticing him noticing. A bland, lined, grey face, dead eyes, toad eyes. Eyes painted on. A squashed toad mouth that found everything wanting.

April shifted upright in her blue seat, turning. He clenched his pencil, and the throbbing subsided into a sulking disquiet. The Substitute Mister handed out two sign-in sheets and pens at each end of the front row. He took up the white cursor then began to draw: Mr...

A white sheet appeared over Ismael's shoulder with a blue-capped Bic. He drew Ismael_Canul in a single calligraphic line without lifting the point. They were looking at each other, muffled giggles, as he handed them forward. Then,

—Eww, it's warm.

She held the pen out. Mocking, feigned grimaces. Conspiring, April said,

—What was he doing with it?

Neither looked at him; he wasn't there. She passed April the paper and the warm pen. Another *eww*.

Ismael wasn't going to cry. He swallowed it down with the wet lumps of yellow, brown, and green. He should've stayed in the middle.

Don't forget that face. Her face. It was only a surface. No one was solid unless he sculpted them with his own hands.

White lines on the black plane, a geometry simpler than what he was looking for, but a building block. Like LEGOs. Like bricks in the wall. Like letters in a word – the language of surfaces.

He looked again. Along the complex curves of April's foot, half in its shoe, the rosy highlights of her sole, it resurged. Biting his underlip, he looked at the white lines on black, an eggshell structure from the side.

Something turned over in his gut. Want. Frustration, a wet, sour lump, but he swallowed it.

He looked past her.

T   he metal tube stank of green vinyl, foam, and
black rubber. It was a relief to step out into the
green air. Yellow and black, warning colours;
on black rubber, it trailed black soot.

I'll walk with you, Sophie says.

Curved black strips carved through the green, striped
with yellow dashes down their centres. Warning colours.
The happy trees were spaced apart like the large boxes
separated by wood slats and covered in wood slats.
White, red, and blue irregular pentagons. Flag colours.
Some flags.

In the City Of, the strips were small and twisted,
cracked and divoted. The boxes were taller and pressed
closer together, the cars jammed everywhere. Here, each
box had its own dead end, perpendicular to the strip. It
was quiet. In the City Of, there was always something
shrill. Something screaming.

It's like there's no one else here, Sophie says.

But there were cars in their dead ends. Behind the
horizontal slats, behind the unshuttered glass, they were
there. Or they weren't till you opened the door. There
was no way to be sure – there was nothing solid.

It's like ghosts, he says. They're kind of there even
when you can't see them.

Creepy. So, if there's, like, five billion of them out
there, but we can't see them, then the whole wide world
is haunted, right? Are we ghosts, too?

How would we know?

Which house is yours?

The small red one.

The red house was a pentagonal prism like most of
the wooden boxes. It had the same lawn as the house
next door, but he only mowed inside the white slats.

Which room is yours? she asks.

Around the left side, the corner in back.

Wait, she says as he opens the gate, when will you draw me?

Maybe later. I have homework.

The door was never locked. He could hear the screaming before he opened it. The smaller ones couldn't play without screaming. The walls were papered with squiggly lines, and the small ones crayoned across them. Mixed media.

Matchbox cars were scattered over long woodgrain tiles. A metal shell on top and plastic on the bottom, they flexed when you squeezed them. Hollow, too.

Timmy couldn't keep his shirt on, bashing two cars together while droning aloud. The oval edge of the opening in his back was thinner than paper. As thin as light.

The reversed contours of his chest and belly were defined by shadows, the arm holes pitch black without a flashlight. Not peach-cream like his skin, but a seamless titanium-white. Like the shiny paint of a brand-new car with a sticker on the glass.

No one was looking at the flickering cube on one side of the space. A living room, where the bulbous cube played out life on one bowed glass side. And there, on that curved surface, Nancy's soaps and War in Iraq were solid.

He'd asked the Science Mister about mirrors and lenses, about how they created an image. The Science Mister had talked about advanced placement.

Ismael went to his room. There were three small ones, and they weren't allowed inside. They shared a room upstairs near Frank and Nancy. The bigger two had their own rooms, too. There were always six from the System.

On his file, he was a number. They all were, and the red house was a middle place, not a «home» like they called it. A home business. The older ones would have to leave soon; then, he would be next.

It was the same colour as the lunch plates: «Eggshell», Nancy had said to his question. There were images taped up on the walls, «bands», her word. Pink Floyd. Led Zeppelin. They'd been here when he'd arrived, and he left them up. He was ready to go anytime.

On the small desk, his *Appleseed* books. The rest of his lawnmower money. He had volumes one and two. Three was next year, or shell out for the back issues. A ruined world of computers and machines. Their future. The machines were very detailed, but he had to do his own designs. Not copy.

Ismael sat on the bed. He had take-home tests: Geometry. Social. French. It was part of the routine. Maybe later.

He took the pad and pencil from his bookbag. He sketched two light ovals, intersecting, then shorter ob-longs, a row of small circles. Then he began to connect the shapes, a heavier line to define April's foot. To make it solid. The shading would come last, but he stalled on the smaller details. The exact shape of the nails, the contours of her toes... The details were fuzzy, but then, he couldn't remember the colour of her eyes either.

He couldn't use his own foot for reference. It wasn't even close.

His door didn't lock, but they usually didn't barge in. It was still a risk. He slipped off of the bed and reached between the box spring and mattress. He slipped out a crinkled, brown paper bag.

Inside were two glossies. One was *Entertainment for Men* from Jake, the bigger boy. The other was *Fashion* but titled in French. Addressed to Nancy on a white label, he'd lifted it from the mail. The first showed everything; the second, even more.

They were magnetic and repellant, from glossy covers to glossy pages. He'd shuddered the first time, running his fingers over solid torsos, the line of the spine going down. Over the ripples of muscle and bone, but the paper was smooth and cold. The camera adds ten pounds, he'd heard them say. Even they knew there was a difference.

Was it the lens? The interpretative surface that made three dimensions two, making hollow solid? He'd looked for books at the library but hadn't asked the librarian. Nor had he talked to the Science Mister or the Math Mizz about looking at three dimensions from two. They would bring up advanced placement.

The one «for men» didn't show them much. The other, here and there. He found the pose he needed. That picture: in the blue dress. Curly dark hair, red smiling lips, her legs bare from the knee down. Not crossed, but at the correct angle, away from him. The first time he'd looked at it – entranced, looking at them, something had spotted his briefs.

He compared the sketch. Of course, April's wasn't the model's. But there were clues, reminders, and inspiration. It responded again, but he focused on the dulling pencil tip, its drag on the white paper. On the manifold of grey lines, till a sharp *wrap! wrap!* on glass.

A small white fist. He flips the pad and hides the glossies. Looking up on the other side of the glass, Sophie. The window lifts with a wood-on-wood groan.

Help me up, Sophie says.

Why are you… ?

You said you'd draw me.

Okay, he says, then helps her up and over the window sill. She says, Where should I sit?

Wherever, he says, shrugging.

You were drawing on your bed? I'll sit in the chair.

Sophie pulls the chair away from the small desk and rotates it toward the narrow bed. She sits and asks, What were you drawing?

Nothing, he says. He flips to a blank page and shifts to the edge of the mattress.

How should I pose?

Take off your shoes. And socks.

Should I take off anything else?

No.

Sophie unlaces her white canvas sneakers, Superga, and unrolls her white socks.

Put them up on the edge of the chair, then spread your fingers on your insteps.

She draws up her legs, then rests her head between her knees. She says, Fingers and toes?

They're the hardest to draw, he says. And noses. Look over there.

She turns her head. A three-quarter profile. He roots in his bag for the pencil sharpener, then flips to a fresh sheet. He starts over.

The light changes, and he hesitates over the shadows. He rubs his fingertip, dented by the pencil. A solid hexagon.

What would it take to make Sophie solid? Not just in clay or marble, but moving and talking like the «Gunslinger». With pistons, wires, and gears. Like that.

Is it done? Sophie asks.

There was a knock at the door.

—Yes, he said.

It swung open. Nancy said,

—Have you finished your homework?

—Not yet.

She stepped into the room. Her straight, dark bowl-cut hair, her surface leathery and lined. She was taller than him but not by much; she looked at his pad upside down.

—Your drawings are very good, but you do have to finish your homework. Is that a friend from school?

—No; I made her up.

—Come to the kitchen; we need to talk before dinner.

—Okay.

He left it where it was and followed. Two of the three small ones were seated on the floor, watching lines move on the curved glass. Drawings were always solid, even when they moved. Even when they sang «Row row row your boat» and changed the words. High RPM

record player voices. The Chipmunks' Life is just a dream.
Timmy bashed yellow plastic trucks in the corner, a
white hole flickering with the bulb.

The kitchen smelled like the school cafeteria. Boiled
greens and tomato sauce: a casserole and broccoli.
Hamburger Helper.

Frank had a big, lumpy nose, his surface carved with
drooping hangdog lines. The kitchen floor was linoleum, a carved grid. In art, they'd carved white linoleum
with channel knives. Grooved the surfaces to print
on another surface. Frank's buttoned-up shirts were
printed with lines like the wallpaper.
—Nancy, close the door. Izzy, we got a call from your
school counsellor today. He said your art teacher talked
to him about a painting you did for class. He was con-
cerned. Frank nodded as he talked, agreeing with
himself:—Look, Izzy, we have a lot of experience working with the System. You have to play along. Tell 'em
what they want to hear. You didn't ask to be in the game,
but you are, and you're starting with a handicap. Don't
tell anybody I said that, but you are ¶. Right now, the
cards are against you. You're behind the curve. They're
looking for any reason to sideline you, and you can't
give them one. You know what you're supposed to say,
what they expect, amirite? I don't have to tell you. When
they ask you to draw a family. You know what to do.

Ismael said,
—They threw me away.

They left me to die, he didn't say.
—And if you get stuck on that, Frank said, that's where
you'll end up again. The System doesn't forgive. If you
say or do anything they don't like, they'll get rid of
you ¶. Your file will get lost, your application thrown
away. They'll erase you ¶. Everything is part of the System. Everything ¶. You're smarter than the others, and
that makes it harder. You want to question things. Play
ball instead ¶. When other people clap, you clap. When
other people smile, you smile.

—You want me to pretend.
—Every single day. From when you wake up until you
go to bed. You have to fool everybody. If somebody asks
how you are, you say good. Not fine.
—No, Nancy said. You're doing great.
—Don't do it for us, Frank said, or because we told you
to. Do it for you ¶. You're from Belize. You were never
homeless. Your parents are gone. You have a foster family. That's how you say it ¶. Family, not just parents.

   You had to be precise with the System, like filling in
those little ovals on a test. No. 2 only. Keep it inside the
lines.

   Ismael said okay to everything.

   Jake met him in the hallway.
—Hey, 'lil dude. I'm gonna need that back.
—Okay, Ismael said.

   He didn't mind; he didn't need that. He gave that back
first, then closed his door, then sat on the bed.

   Sophie says, Why did they throw you away?

   I could see through them.

   You're not like them.

   You don't know that. There's no way to know.

   They know you're different.

   These? On the surface. They don't see anything else.

   What you do matters. They just warned you. The
System.

   I can only do what they tell me. Only say what they
tell me. It's the same as telling me to disappear.

   Maybe it's like that for them. Think about it. They
had to choose, too.

   «Be an architect; be an engineer». They already chose
for me.

   You can do it, though. That's what they're saying.

   They're tying my hands.

   You have to take control – tell them you want to be an
artist. You can't stay here.

   I'll be out there, alone. Again.

   He takes a deep breath. A deep sigh.

She says, If things were different, could it have been you and me? Us?

No, he says. You'd be just like them.

A white hole, she whispers. Like that bitch in French.

Like April, he didn't say. And now I have to be like them, too. The surface they want to see. Whether I am or not.

She shakes her head with a sad smile and reddened eyes. Hide, she says. Hide under their noses, but don't be empty. Never be empty. Promise me.

He considers. He can't see it – doesn't know what it means – but he says, If there is a way, I'll find it.

His drawing of her was solid. She wouldn't just disappear.

Ismael picked up the pencil. He had an idea.

Serret, Never Human,
III.

T hou feeſt, we are not all alone vnhappie:
This wide and vniuerſall Theater
Preſents more wofull then the Sceane
Wherein we play in.

ISMAEL
All the world's a ſtage
And all the men and women meerely Players:
The haue their Exits and their Entrances;
And one man in his time playes many parts,
His Acts being ſeven ages. At firſt, the Infant,
Mewling, and puking in the Nurſes armes.
Then, the whining Schoole-boy, with his Satchell,
And ſhining morning face, creeping like ſnaile
Vnwillingly to ſchoole.

The chorus laughed. The English Misses asked,
—And what does that mean to you, Ishmael?
—That everything's made up. It's all fake. Everyone is
pretending.
    The chorus laughed again. The English Misses asked,
—Anyone else? Johnathan.
—That everyone has a place in the world. That we all go
through the same stuff.
—Very good. The human condition. You'll hear this…
    Ismael knew better, but no one would listen. Except
the System, and every answer was a test. Frank and
Nancy weren't wrong.
    He was in, or he was out. With every 0, he was
downgraded. He'd pass through with every 1. April was
up front, so he'd moved to the back. Away from her and
her 1s. She was still pretty… on the surface. It was like
two magnets when turned the other way.
    But it was becoming clearer: a sorting program.

Habitual 0s sat in the back till they were sorted out and collected into different routines. Put on different tracks.

The Homeroom Misses had told him he wasn't in trouble, but he had to see the Counselling Mister after English. Unlike French or Latin, English wasn't about English. He had to read *Webster's New World Pocket Dictionary* and *The Elements of Style* for himself. Red, white and blue, two old books left behind by whoever had left the posters behind. Or someone before them – someone else from the System.

A noose was snugged up around the Counselling Mister's neck. The flat belt of blue hung down over the buttons of his button-up. The Principals wore nooses, too. And the talking busts on that glass screen. Tight under their collars, nooses ensured their hollows would never show and hid the buttoned seam down their front. Nothing to see here.

The Counselling Mister's hair was neatly parted on one side. His mouth curved a lot, but his eyes didn't change behind his thin, wire-rimmed spectacles.
—Given where you're coming from – and there's no shame in that. But given that, your foster parents asked for extra guidance into what's expected of you ¶. We want you to know that you have many options. It can be more difficult for gifted children to fit in, but we don't want you to feel disadvantaged in any way ¶. You've been recommended for Honours Math. We'd normally wait till next semester, but we're prepared to move you mid-term. You'll have to work hard to catch up, but I'm sure you can do it ¶. And the sooner you are on the AP track, the better. You'll be the first Hispanic student to take AP Trigonometry at West. Do you think you're ready?

Track was a word Ismael had already flagged.
—Do I have to decide now?
—No, but the sooner you get onto your track, the better. Some people will tell you that you don't have to decide now, that you can wait for college to find yourself. That

might be okay for average students without intellectual curiosity or personal drive. But to reach for the highest track, we should prepare you now ¶. The worst thing we could do is leave you unchallenged. You could become bored, even drop out.

—I get it.

—The sooner you have an idea of what you'd like to accomplish in the future, the sooner we can get you on track to succeed. While most of our students go to West, you can apply to East or even look into a scholarship at a private academy ¶. West has the superior Art program and a good range of AP courses, but East focuses on college prep. It also has a challenging IB diploma program, and you may qualify for exam fee waivers. Is there anything you've thought about?

The Art Misses had talked about West and art schools. He'd listened.

—I've already decided.

The Counselling Mister leaned forward, picking up his pen.

—Excellent! What were you thinking of?

—I'm going to build robots. Like in the movies, but better.

—That's exactly what I like to hear. Something ambitious. Like computers, robotics will be important in the future. You've seen how the automotive industry uses robots to make cars?

—A little. I looked for books on it, but the library doesn't have any.

—Proactive. You have a bright future if we can channel those energies productively. I'll put Robotics Engineer as your career goal ¶. There are no guarantees, but you should set your aim high: the major technical schools. MIT. Caltech. Graduate studies, I assume?

—Whatever it takes.

—Are you willing to give up access to the Art program at West?

—Yes. IB at East, you said?

—I'll make some calls. As long as you apply yourself, I think we can make it happen. Your GPA is critical going forward, not just in Honours Math but across the board. You'll need to take every subject seriously and have high participation ¶. Avoid spreading yourself too thin with unneeded electives. Honours English, for example, can wait until you're at East, and then you can decide to keep French or Latin for your IB. You will need one of them ¶. Extracurriculars will become unavoidable once you're there, too. But for now, let's focus on bringing your GPA up to a three-point-nine by the end of next year. Study and homework need to be an everyday habit. Attendance, perfect if possible. Think of a missed day as a handicap on your GPA ¶. What you do today determines your doctorate a dozen years from now and the rest of your future. It's hard when you're eleven or twelve to think about where you'll be in your twenties. But the clearer your goal is to you, the easier it will be to do what's needed every day in order to succeed. «The journey of a thousand miles begins with a single step» – it's an old saying from the Far East. We'll start you in Honours Math next week.

Ismael said okay to everything and took mental notes. It was the machinery of the System. The right routines to get on the right track through the right programs. From middle place to middle place, the steps of a pyramid leading up and up and up. One mistake and you'd get stuck or fall down.

For most, their track kept them on the level they were born into. Most climbers failed, and falling off your track left you on a lower step or back where he'd begun. He'd seen it all from the gutter. Those who'd fallen, those who broke. Those who disappeared.

It was a glimpse into the source code of the sorting program. The acronyms and keywords. *Success*. That's how he would have to talk, too. *Good*, not *okay*, like Frank said.

He walked the deserted circuit, bookbag on one shoulder, blue pass in hand. In a way, it was worse than

being out there. Harsher. Colder. There was no place for
him, not as himself.

The pass crumpled. With the right surface, he would
pass through. He grimaced at a sinking nausea.

He smoothed the pass and handed it to the Science
Mister. He sat on the front row next to April. He was
still looking ten or twelve years ahead, at how old he'd
be then – at what he'd be doing. The middle places
looked smaller if you were stepping over them.

The science routine was easy, and he usually input
the 1s when it stalled. At the head of the class, there was
no need to look to his sides. No need to look back.

He didn't look forward to Gym. To the locker room,
to the white holes. He didn't mind swimming, but
watching the water swirl around their emptiness… He
focused on his stroke, on his breathing. The Gym
Mister had talked about the swim team; if not here,
then at West.

Maybe at East, if that's what it took. If he had the
stomach for it. He didn't have the stomach for lunch
and went to the library. It was quiet.

You're not going to eat? Sophie says.

Not hungry.

Are you sure about this?

Lunch? he says.

About giving up art. It's all you have.

I'm not giving up art. I'm going to make machines
that *are* art.

It's not the same. You won't be an artist.

I'll be an engineer, like they said.

For me? She spreads her hands in front of him. For
this?

What I engineer will be art. You.

I'm afraid. I'm afraid you won't be able to turn back.

I can't. I'm on a track, like a train. As soon as I left
that office.

Can you even make something real after you become
a liar? After you spend twenty or thirty years as a liar?

Everything I need to know is behind their doors, and

they can lock me out. They don't want to see me – they want to see what they want to see – like the school counsellor. They used to try so hard not to see me that they would actually step on me while I was sleeping. They'd stand on me like I wasn't even there. Or like it didn't matter, like I was trash on the sidewalk. If I said anything, they would just look at me with these dead eyes they have and not even move their foot. Like Frank and Nancy said, there's no other way.

And it's making you sick to your stomach.

I'll get used to it.

And then, what kind of monster will you make?

Like in the movies, but better.

It's too late to save you.

I decided yesterday.

Why, she asks, because you had a wet dream?

The spasms had lifted him to consciousness under a puddle, her face a lingering spectre.

That's not the reason

Yes, it is.

Those other kids will join the Army, or work at a supermarket, or go to jail. I've heard all the stories. I won't be like them.

The next program wasn't part of what he would build. But it was part of his track, and he had to «play ball», as Frank said. Play along for a 3.9. If it was a pyramid with four steps, it was too late to reach the peak. Here, but not at East. Not at the middle place after that. There was still a chance. Ismael could still do it.

3.9 came first. He moved through the circuit with purpose. He sat on the front row – at the end, the last at the head of the class, for now.

The Social Mister had hair around his jaw and chin. Most of the misters didn't. He called out a series of names. Alphabetically, by the names he didn't say. Called him Ishmael.

—Here.

—Ah, I didn't see you on that side. How're you?

—Good.

The names went on. Ismael could say good and not okay and didn't feel anything. He could say it to Ishmael and not complain. He could play ball.

Sophie sits on the grey carpet, legs and arms crossed. Red around her eyes. She doesn't say anything. She watches him input 1s, then passes him a note.

He unfolds it: WHAT A BIG NOSE YOU HAVE.

I'm busy, he scrawls on the other side and gives it back.

She pens another line and makes a football fold. She tosses it onto his open history book: IS IT WORSE TO BE HOLLOW OR TURN TO WOOD?

He writes back, Better wood or metal or even mud than hollow.

She writes for a long time on the back of the un-folded sheet, then back on the front. He takes notes and inputs 1s. Participation.

Sophie refolds it back in on itself, inside out. Another lob, then she stalks out. No return address.

The black ink riding blue lines, her round and bubbly letters were big and small this time:

A boy dreamed of a girl, but she wasn't real.

The boy was real, but the Devil said, I can make you a deal, and one day, boy, you'll be able to make a metal girl. The Devil wore a tie and glasses and had a magic pen, but the Devil said, You can't sign 'cause a boy's soul don't belong to hisself. But Them, Them offered me the boy's soul. Caesar gave them silver, and they polished Caesar's fine silver. And Them told the boy his flesh 'n' blood was bought 'n' sold, but there was one more thing to sell. Sell it, boy, Them tells him, and we'll sign on the dotted line. It's all you gots left. The Devil is waiting.

The boy longed for the dream and told the Devil, Take this no-good soul. And the boy became cold, stiff, and shiny all over. A clockwork boy full of gears and springs. His nose is a yard long but doesn't get bigger 'cause he can only tell lies. And when he moves, it winds his spring, and the wheels go tick tick tick 'cause wooden boys don't need no heart.

Many years passed, and the wooden boy built the metal girl. He filled her with gears and springs that go tick tick tick 'cause metal girls don't need no heart. The metal girl walked and talked. She was solid and strong. But neither had a soul. Neither had a dream. And the wooden boy couldn't remember if he'd been real after all.

Ismael tucks it away. There was no way to know. Not for sure. Either way, he'd had to choose today. The pointer on the wall clock never stopped stepping: tick, tick, tick. Not even for the buzzer.

It wasn't hard to imagine the best case. Or possibilities that might exceed what he could imagine right now. But the worst case was another shadow that moved with the light. It would cling to everything he did along every step of the program.

Programming was on the third level of the circuit. Grey spaces for his next year, the last year in this middle place. Some of them were bigger, some weren't. He might be, maybe later.

A bigger one asked him,

—What's your name, 'lil dude?

—Ismael.

The bigger one laughed and punched another bigger one in the shoulder.

—Hey, it's the guy from Moby Dick! Ishmael, dude.

—Ishmael, what's up?

The other bigger one extended his hand. Ismael had seen the routine many times. He input 1s: extending his own hand, sliding it back against the other, then bumping fists. He said,

—Not much.

—Hey, this 'lil dude is cool.

He passed the routine and got into the waiting space. It was more blue than grey. The surfaces were arranged in rings rather than rows, the seats facing the walls. On

each surface, two stacked beige boxes. The bottom one
was slotted. The upper was oblong and tilted on a lily
pad. Its front was curved glass: a black screen with green
letters. It made no sounds other than hiss! whirr! or beep!

A beige brick was wired to the bottom box. It was
covered in teeth lettered in black. It was all beige, the
colour of plastic flesh. The teeth clicked when you
pressed them. Something like the slotted box would
have to fit inside the metal girl.

Sophie says, You hated that.

I don't care.

Yes, you do

I won't. I'll get used to it.

And your heart?

Don't need one. I'm ticking fine.

He looks at her. I am going to do it. It can be done,
and I'll be the first.

Do you think she'll thank you?

He stops to think about it. A solid metal girl waking
up. No, he says. Art never thanks the artist.

W   hy did you hollow the back of the torso?
The model was a bare pink superfice. Prone on a sheeted platform, brassy hair woven up. The thinness of her shell was dramatised by her complete exposure, as was the blank whiteness within. A deceptive fragility: she wouldn't crack apart like an empty egg. No matter how you divided them, there was always a surface.

His miniature in clay *was* inaccurate. As thin as he'd made it, clay couldn't represent the zero-pixel superfice. It had no thickness, only the illusion caused by the colour contrast.

Ismael hadn't spoken of it in years: the white holes. This was a transgression, a test.

The cragged furrow of her brow, the pinch of pursed lips. Did the Art Mizz see but disavow? There was still no way to be sure, but every other clay torso had the normal, closed back he also saw now, with his spectacles on. With his *corrected* vision. With them tipped down, the illusion broke, like 3D glasses.

—Even naked, he said, you can show a façade.

—You might add something to clarify. As it is, some might say it's misogynistic.

—I hadn't thought of that.

He hadn't; hollowness wasn't gendered.

—I'll see what I can come up with.

She nodded, then moved on. He was in the wrong major to be in the room. Lesser than.

Sculpture III. It was his last chance to build this part of his skill set under professional guidance. After this, he'd be on his own.

The model was encircled by wooden tripods, grey with old dust. A dozen lumps of grey drawing different solids from the superfice. Next, moulds, then plaster.

He was building *Peter's Gate* for his final: set on three

steps, the seven terraces cut into the inner door case. A
scaled-down complement to Rodin's *Porte L'enfer*.

Ismael had only one angel, and she would be solid,
too. In plaster till he could afford a bronze cast in «your
future».

The System was a game, and he'd learned to score.
Chinos. Oxford cloth button-downs. Penny loafers.
Presentation was part of the GPA, part of the code.
Dress for your English Honours. There was nothing of
him in it. Even his neat side-parted hair, straight out of
Esquire. 3.92 was the floor. His sleeves were rolled up.

He was outside of this program. They coded *bohe-
mian* on a different track. All the same. *Individuality*
and *self-expression* were tests of conformity – of group
self-selection. The key to access or exclusion. Passing
through on his track meant pushback on theirs, but he
required their tech. The illusion of *belonging* wasn't an
option. Latin Honours on his résumé were.

The walls were white behind the cluttered shelving,
but the air was almost grey with the damp scent of
earth. On the other side of this model and every other,
Liz was at the furthest point from him in the circle.
Whatever the radius, they were always on opposite sides
of the diameter. She was almost as white as the hollow
between them; her black hair presumably resurfaced.
He knew nothing but her appellation. On different
tracks, she was always in his path.

There was no buzzer; the program ended when the
Art Mizz said. He wrapped up his routine.

Brick walls outside were veneered with age and
esteem. Ivied, dingy with historic exhaust soot, the
steep rooves crowned with defunct chimneys. It was all
surface. They called it *prestige*.

The air was neither grey nor green, and blue-white
marble vaulted over it undecided.

Pointed black iron spikes were thrust into the ground
outside the cluster of boxes. Cross-braced and welded
together in a ring of black teeth. An unambigüous

aggression between it and the grey City Of. The green lawns and happy trees were fenced in, protected from what moved outside. Picturesque squatters shooed the pigeons away or threw them crumbs.

To hear them talk, the City Of was the place. The place that mattered. There were other places, they'd said, that they'd put into the books and made part of the tests. He'd lived the streets of the City Of across the river. He'd passed through the green sub-urb at the edge of the greater City Of area.

Belize. The mountains. The Kekchí he might've imagined, and the Aztecas the Spanish lied about. Stories, too, were like walls around the City Of. There were grey spots of the City Of scattered all over, they'd said, but he'd only seen the pictures in solid 2D.

He zipped up his jacket for the walk to the next building. Fall began his final cycle at this middle place. A senior again, but for the last time. Every middle place after this would be graduate. He'd take that at one go, ready to get on with «your future».

The leaves had fallen, but snow was a ways off. Many were only wearing sweaters or shirtsleeves between buildings. Pretending to be cold or pretending to not be cold. It was little different from the first middle place. Long and short hairs clustered together or apart in hostile groups of common fear.

It's not too late to change your mind, Sophie says. A supercomputer won't fit inside a humanlike body, and even if it could, there's no battery that could power it. And your theory isn't going to work. It's over.

She is as naked as the model, but the cold only touches the jewellike blue of her eyes. She turns her back on him, an empty white hole, saying, I was never more than this. She looks over her shoulder, Make a plaster girl, then let it go.

I'll make a plaster girl, he says, probably several, but this isn't even the beginning. I'm just warming up. I'll prove my theory works and bring it to realisation.

No one will go along with it. It will cost millions, maybe more. You can't even attempt it by yourself.

That's why I have to go to the next place. So that they'll listen.

He was less than a surface to them. Belize equated *Hispanic* and/or *Latino*, whatever they meant. A statistical percentage for their programs. Accepted without acceptance. Coding let him blend in and pass through, but the System would acknowledge his *pieces of paper*.

There was a gap in his program – a free period. The library was as loud as a café, and it was more productive to wait in the Centre's atrium than in its café.

English was still required. They still didn't teach it unless you asked for a tutor downstairs. But then, French was no longer about French but in French. He filled a wooden chair in the atrium.

He worked on his French. The skill had paid dividends during his internship in the City Of pee-smelling streets and dog-shit sidewalks. At least in the effort, if not the Spanish accent that coloured his French but not his English.

—Heyyy, said Liz, slowing to a stop. They call you Ishmael?

They opened their routines with two or three variations of the same line. It might've been interesting to track the distribution. He made no corrections. She didn't wait for one:

—What was she saying about your piece?

—That it's misogynist.

—How?

—The torso is hollow. I was making a statement about how someone can be superficial even without clothes.

—Don't change it. Call it, *Bitches be fake!*

He shook his head.

—You might be able to get away with that, not me.

—Are you saying that our lovely professor is a hypocritical fake cunt like your piece?

—Exactly.

Her lips were full but not artificial, and she smiled a snarly, asymmetric half-smile. She sat on the wide flat of the armrest, pressing his arm.

—How come I've only seen you in sculpture classes?
—I'm in Engineering with a special concentration in Mechatronics. But my Secondary is Studio Art, so that I could take all those sculpture classes.
—Fuck, you're Leonardo Da Vinci. But you have to paint, too, man!
—I haven't since High School.
—See, you're ruining it. What about next year?
—I've applied to a few places, but ideally down by the Charles. They have a graduate polymers program at their ME school. We'll find out in March.

He didn't mention the joint MBA. He would have to master and control numbers to make it happen.

Liz said,
—No wayyy. That's not Da Vinci at all. C'mon, man...
—For me, it IS an art degree.
—That's shit.

She didn't miss a beat. He said,
—What are you doing next year?

Liz fished inside her droopy black bag and slapped a business card onto the left page of his open book. Red, yellow, and blue bleeding together, her fingernails lacquer black.
—I'm getting a studio, and I'll have my first opening before you know it. I'll make art.

He didn't ask who'd be paying for the studio.
—So will I.
—You need a PhD in plastic to make art? Get a paintbrush.

There was no advantage in going past an M.Sc, but he didn't get into it.
—Polymers will form the structural basis for Bio-mimetic Robotics. Androids and things like that. It's already being researched in prosthetics, and I expect the two fields will end up very close together. Like in sci-fi.

42

—Androids aren't art. Don't be goofy.

—Mine will be. When I say polymer, I don't mean plastic like a Barbie doll. Human skin is a polymer ¶. Imagine if Rodin had to invent a new type of bronze. I have to get my hands into the medium I'm going to sculpt with.

She leant back, frowny face, then closer.

—I get you, I guess. She made a show of thinking, eyes away, brown eyes, then:—Where'd you get those glasses?

—Paris.

—And what're you even reading? In French, right? I thought you were Hispanic.

The System required him to be. Only native Americans from the north were Native American. If you were from the south of the border, you were other. He'd taken advantage of it to get into this program; it was all numbers. He played ball.

—More or less, he said, shrugging. It says, «Tridimen-sionnalité du simulacre – pourquoi le simulacre à trois dimensions serait-il plus proche du réel que celui à deux dimensions?»

Cocked eyebrow,

—Come again?

—Baudrillaud is talking about holograms. He asks, «Why would a three-D hologram be closer to reality than a two-D one?»

—But we are three dimensions.

—Are you sure? Maybe we've been fooled.

Liz laughed, then spread her hands, saying,

—Or we've tricked ourselves, right? We're like Ancient Egyptian art, but our brains interpret it the other way. And in the real world, we have outlines instead of shadows.

—Exactly.

—We should hang out. Text me, she said, standing, don't call.

Skinny jeans, Converse hi-tops, big feet, but she was legit tall. She headed for the stairs up as if he were intended to watch her ascent and the fit of her jeans

from behind. Her number was on the card. He wedged
it in with his polished brass bookmark.

Sophie says, See? There's another way.

She's no different than the others.

She is.

I can see through her.

You haven't.

I would.

You're not nothing. Can't that be enough?

You don't want me to pretend – then, you want me to
pretend.

Are you pretending? Were you pretending to look at
her like that? The way you have been?

I've been pretending for longer than I can remember
now. Why add to it?

Sophie crosses her arms and says, You're throwing
away the real for the impossible.

He closes the book.

—You have to have something before you can throw it
away.

His words rang hollow in the empty atrium. Footfalls
echoed on the stairs. Hard and soft soles. Then, an
inrush of voices: the next wave.

He did have to go and go through the motions
again. It was the same old echo routine. The shorter
hairs had, on average, gotten taller. An eggshell room,
a rectangular plane, wood grain, circled by short grey
chairs. Rectangles or circles sometimes replaced rows.
The same book bags. The same black plane on one side,
above a metal tray of cursors.

They'd entered the space and sat without seeing it,
walking while staring at or typing on their handheld
monoliths. Clarke and Kubrick's portent of change,
but no one was radioing Jupiter. They were bowed over
them, gripped, even seated together. Little talking or
teasing. They were all connected but not together.

He kept his monolithic cellular radio, more microlith,
in his pocket and worked on his French.

44

You can see the puppet strings, Sophie says. Cut your
losses and pick a different goal. Go after her.

He says, There's nothing else in front of me.

You'll turn into that old man in Metropolis.

Which one?

The childless one. Who else?

I'm not building a surrogate for a dead woman.

No, a surrogate for one who never lived.

My work will transcend anything I imagined as a
kid. Whatever I can imagine now. Even a muse is only a
starting point; I am not limited to you.

And the wooden boy said, I'll never change! 'Cause
he'd forgotten what it was to have a soul. He was right:
wooden boys always stay the same.

Ismael scratched his nose. It wouldn't get any shorter.
The English Mister was short:

—Everyone should be prepared to discuss the reading.

Ismael switched books for a portrait of an artist
who didn't paint, sculpt, or draw. This artist wandered
around off-track with no progression and no goal, like a
homeless guy.

Laptops folded open like domino chips, leaping
upright. A division between the whites and the greys.
Here, almost all white, but in the engineering labs, all
grey. White-chinned microliths tracked against the
all-black.

His notes tracked 80% biography, 20% dated German
philosophy and psychology. English was mentioned
once regarding its historicity. The holder of the English
publication rights had listed it in the most important
novels of the past century. #5 of 100. You had to sell the
idea before you could print the books.

He had to sell his ideas to the jackets and nooses that
controlled the numbers. For them to cede control to
him. He had to dazzle them with his white pieces of
paper; he had to learn their codes. It was clear he'd have
to be at the forefront.

Transmitting to who-knew-where, they got into their

glassy radios before before packing up. He led the way out, then descended the stairs in the momentary silence.

It might very well be that a muse could become an obstacle, obstructing his vision. Had it been anything but the mirror of his doubt?

He spotted her again: Liz, going up the library stairs, two other longer hairs in formation. She didn't look back.

Serret, Never Human,
V.

L iz is *naked*, standing over him. She presses one
foot to his face, toenails piano-black. Her skin
is immaculate, white against her black hair.
Harder, the pad of her foot against his cheek, she turns
his face this way, then that. Her toes move down over
his nose, his lips, and into his mouth.

The ceiling was white. He blinked at the red digits:
eight minutes till the alarm. He flipped the switch. No
spill, but his unassuaged rigidity didn't subside. He'd
pulled her shirt free and run his hands over her voidless
skin. Given that, was it even her?

It was up to him to descend from the hyperreal to the
real – from the hollow to the solid.

Unlike the room at the red house, there'd been
no collage of images on the greenish eggshell walls
when he'd moved in. The green shade of some fresh
duck eggs he'd seen at the green market. Unlike the
room at the red house, this space was divided: two
beds, two chairs, and two small desks. The other half,
Artic Monkeys, *Muse*. A clutter of nonessentials that
glossed the performative surface. As such, they were
indispensable.

His half, a curated disorder. *Kind of Blue* and a *Jazz
Festival* he'd never been to. A handful of used CDs he'd
never played. He only had to wear headphones to be left
alone, big bulky German ones with a black coiled cord.

He'd hacked the code: wear the emperor's clothes.
The middle three volumes of *La Recherche*. *Godard* and
Bazin. Nothing anyone on the Engineering track or the
other side of the room would dig into. Things only grey
hairs talked about: esteemed but unassailable, opti-
mised to pass through.

The morning routine didn't change, like his unmade
bed. His beard was light, but he shaved every day.
He left no variable unchecked. He wound his watch,

Speedmaster Professional, by hand, the slow beat of a
clockwork heart. Its patina of age was older than he was.
It was unnecessary and a vital gesture. One point in the
constellation that let them tell a story to themselves.

In reflexion, a construction as precise as any autom-
aton from the 17th-century atelier of Jaquet-Droz. His
closet: an even number of button-downs in different
colourways. A few pairs of the same chinos. Two
colourways of the same shoes. But with an overt quirk
memorable enough to #individual.

His face had hollowed in recent years, and some of
the longer hairs had commented on his cheekbones.
«Exotic», they'd said a few times to each other in his
hearing. They didn't do anything else; they were all talk.
Empty words.

The years of book study had led to spectacles and
relief from the glare of white holes. Taking advantage
of his proximity for the summer, he'd gone to Bonnet
first. It was a two-month wait for a pair of tortoiselook
'65 Corbu frames. They'd recommended a gradient
rose tint for computer glare *and* for the look. A layer
of «opacité et réserve», they'd said. A new signature
distraction and a new icebreaker. Something else for
them to say besides «Call you Ishmael?»

To pass through, one had to resolve the contradic-
tion: fit in but stand out. To achieve his ambition, he'd
have to become an engineer with the stature of an
architect. *Ismael Canul* would have to become a brand.

He was neatly overdressed for his part-time at the
green market, but he couldn't afford laxity. You never
knew whom you might encounter on the red train there
and back or who might walk in while he was working.
Truth – their word – was a mask worn even in private.
While only the internships went on his LinkedIn, he
needed numbers for his radio microlith, &c., during the
school year. Scholarships, internships, and loans didn't
cover everything. The numbers were significant.

He paused over the threshold, ears ringing with

the rare silence. One foot on either side. There is no shadow, no whisper. No glint of blonde hair, no flash of blue eye. No snide remark, no warning. He closed the door.

Those from a higher step were still inactive or out. He walked to the starfish-shaped Square – it was always moving. It was cold cold this early, grey light under the grey upside-down sea. Cars trailed fading wisps of cloud. His clouds preceded him. Only those on the lowest step or below the pyramid trafficked the concrete on the weekend's mornings. Grey on grey shadows.

His track was a high wire. If he lost focus, he would go tumbling down. At the Square, a newsstand shelved with papers out of date before they were printed. Just past it, he went under: yellow stripes edging the subway stairs. The green market was at the other end of a red line, a duck pond with bronze ducks and grey pigeons, and a bay with no sea.

Sure, there were garage engineers who'd started up themselves. But, in the end, the System had assimilated them and all of their works. «Don't be evil».

DARPA funding trumped Asimov's laws of robotics, but military drones weren't his track. He was threading a needle.

A white square with red and green printing sat on wooden slats. A half circle of unleavened starch layered with a congealment of vegetable and animal matter. Cold. A dozen years ago, he would've snatched it and looked for a safe spot to eat. It would've been a find. Now, it was a reminder of what waited outside the System. How far he could fall.

The System was in everything.

He'd gone from a nine-digit case number to an eight-digit student and a four-digit employee. Shelve vials of coloured and clear liquids. Stack metal cylinders label front. He was just a pair of hands and a back strong enough to move boxes. Some, like him, were passing through. For others, it was their track.

Up and down the stacks, they pushed green plastic baskets with their elbows. Not woven baskets but injection moulded. Thermoplastics.

Like an autonomous robot operating within its lane but less aware, it wasn't clear if most of them were conscious. Rotating left or rotating right, obstacles appear like surprises. Sorry. Sorry. Sorry, inflexionless soundbite. Add horns, and they'd be cars.

—Do you work here? from behind him.

He's wearing the green apron over his button-down and chinos, the green market logo screened in white. He nodded to the wide deer eyes and raised eyebrows. Fear. Again,

—Do you work here?

—Yes.

—Where are the organic peas?

—You're standing next to them.

—O! Which ones are organic?

He points at the ones marked *organic* in high-contrast letters. Their head jerks back. Surprise, again.

—O! Which is the good one?

He shrugs. They look at him, drooping eyebrows, mouth open. Confusion.

—You don't know?

—No.

—Okaythankyou.

Peering at the labels, they leant forward. Dismissal.

A repeating sub-routine, two or three times a Saturday morning. In time, shelving robots would replace this track. Covered with flashing ads, prepared with recommendations. «Do you work here?» replaced with «Hello?»

He exchanged time for numbers. He would have to work within the constraints of clocks and numbers every day and on every step of «your future». He clocked out for lunch and for the day.

Pieces of paper could represent the numbers, but they weren't the numbers. They were a distraction. A diversion from the real numbers, and they were fiction, too – but a fiction that upheld the System.

The red train was a longitudinal elevator. East–west. He stood still, didn't look at anyone, and descended from -71.080 to -71.119. From the City Of, under the river, under the City Of, to the City Of. Back towards the Square but one stop short. There was standing room and empty, Sophieless seats.

Brunch was when they started *the weekend* on the middle steps. It was a weekly test, a part of his track. The ground-level corner of a concrete cube wasn't shaded by short, fringed blue planes. Mediterranean: Greek and the Near East – which was also the Middle East and Asia West. It wasn't busy.

It was dim inside, lit by indirect sun. Planes empty and clustered were evenly diffused. To the left of the entrance, two rectangular planes had been pushed together, an open grey laptop on one corner. Chairs ringed it like in a classroom.

The twins weren't related. Everyone asked. Overanimated with a heavy hand and narrow lines, they dressed out of his lookbook, except for the sneakers. Engineering track favoured soft shoes. The management track, hard soles, leather. He had no choice but to signal his intentions. Suits-and-nooses were vestments of integration into the System: the control of numbers. Money was numbers; people were numbers. In time, a noose would hang from his neck, too.

They waved him over.

—Dude! You have to hear this story.

—Get this. We were working on the dual-arm robot and kept getting the same four-o-o-eight error. We changed everything: The encoder. All of the sensors. The PCB. The wiring harness. Fucking everything.

—Guess what it was?

Ismael knew he wasn't supposed to guess.

—What?

—The cable.

—One of the pins was broken. We didn't even notice.

They were the first three of eight place settings. The Replicant Alliance. Deez WatchnutZ. Two overlapping Venn circles. Maybe a third.

His cylinder of water smelled like chlorine. He ordered a Turkish IPA, not in the style of India, but of those that had overruled it and allied against Turkey. Irony had a bitter sparkle.

A crowd gathered on the pavement outside, then filed in with the clamour of group myopia. They added a third plane.

The East Asians were called Asians; the South, West, and North Asians weren't. The East Asian percentage was a negative handicap. This much and no more. They'd fallen off their track and landed here. There were pyramids everywhere, but one System.

Some, like him, were climbing up. Within the System but not a part of it. They would climb to different steps on the pyramid. Some would be future leaders in their specialisation.

There were a few tagalongs that didn't say much, and he didn't expect much from them. Devesh led them like a shark. Shaggy-haired, dark brown hands waving with every line, always reaching for connexion. He bumped fists and patted shoulders, a full round of the triple plane, before he sat next to Ishmael. These Asians called him «a golden spoon» behind his back. Devesh said,
—Speedy Pro! What's next on your buy list?
—A Heuer BUND.
—This guy! He's a purist. Look at this: JLC Chocolat. Limited edition. A present from my mother. She has beautiful taste.

A polished pink alloy frame and a dark brown face. 12, and pink metal hash marks. Burgundy belt. Three or four Speedy Pros by the numbers.

Devesh swivelled the clock face in its brancard to display the polished back, then back again. A watch for princes with strings of polo ponies. But he was from

the top step of another pyramid, and he'd come from
the City Of to the City Of to gather his laurels.

—Look at this face, Devesh said to him. Pretty like a
girl. You should grow a beard like me.

—I don't think that's in the cards.

Across the aisle from them, a new clustering was in
progress. On the near parallel, long hair, mid-skirt, her
long legs crossing. Bare feet were staged on the obtuse
slope of pillared planes warped into a complex curve.

Devesh noticed him noticing.

—Vaah, she's hot. Go chat her up.

There was no reason to, but Ismael didn't say that.
That was part of the test.

—She's not that interesting.

—You have to get your dick wet sometimes, bhai. Good
enough is good enough. You don't want to be one of these
guys.

A nontacit reminder that inclusion hung on adher-
ence to expected routines. Ismael couldn't do everything
himself. Turing-level interactive personas, so-called AI,
was a separate discipline from robotics, per se. He'd
have to leave those developments to others, but he
needed to interface with them. To integrate their work
with his.

His senior thesis, An Architecture for Distributed
Semi-Autonomous Robotics, was the foundation of «your
future». An autonomous android with an onboard
neural net and controller was science fiction. Instead
of micronisation, he proposed exploiting advances in
cloud computing and wireless throughput. A wireless
controller and a remote AI agent. Whether on Wi-Fi
or cellular, the humanoid robot would be a battery-
powered drone.

Not everyone agreed:

—No one wants an android drone. C3PO wasn't a drone!

—Nobody wants an android that isn't a drone! said Ismael. Nothing is potentially more dangerous than a
wholly independent robot ¶. Besides, you'll need a

brain the size of one of Google's data centres to run it. Tell me where I'm going to fit that on a five-four chassis with double Ds? Semi-autonomous should be the goal.

He had to sell the idea before he could build the robots. The waiter asked them to keep their voices down, and Devesh laughed at the heated spectacle. He put one hand on Ismael's shoulder.

—This guy is going to work for my company.

—Show me your offer – in writing.

Devesh laughed again. Somehow, without mentioning anime or manga, the twiggy, orange-haired Weeb said,

—You know, Ishmael's got those extra-large glasses like «Tyrell» in *Blade Runner*; he looks expensive. Hire me instead. I'll give you a good deal.

—All of you, Ismael countered, pointing at that side of the plane, are *that* guy, not me. I'm designing the body. The brain is your job.

That got them back into the multimodal argument. He kept his mouth shut and listened. The twins were up and dragged half of the onlookers into the verbal mosh pit:

—What are you talking about? Mixed-modal is the future for all AI, not just robots.

—We can't rely on natural language processing. Yes, it's the next step from text prompts, but the agent needs to be able to infer from what it sees: interpret body language and all the little nonverbal cues. Microëxpressions. All of it. Stop thinking with a terminal.

—But that would be different for every user: we wouldn't be able to implement global policies for vision-language processing. The AI would have to profile individual users.

—Exactly. An agent that adapts to user preferences for *every* individual user.

—What about consciousness? piped in a tagalong.

—That's a problem for cognitive scientists. Any of those here? Show of hands?

It was a joke, but everyone looked around. There weren't any. Devesh noted,

—Is it a good idea? You spend billions and billions developing a synthetic consciousness for broad commercial applications. Then, it applies to the UN for human rights?

Someone whistled.

—So, on the one hand, we need it to be as convincing as possible to the user, but without it going all like, cogito ergo sum on us. Amirite?

—Did we ever want it to act like a real person or better than real?

There were a lot of «better»'s.

—Do you sacrifice suspension of disbelief for usability? Forget Turing?

—Is anyone really intending to make C3PO? Who wants that?

—We're making tools. Robotic servants. Functionality is king.

—Waifus, bro, added the Weeb, arms wide. I'm all about waifus.

Lex was a regular, another one with large spectacles, if less flashy than Ismael's. A quiet one, but when he spoke, everyone listened:

—I get where you guys are coming from, but I have to disagree. By not pursuing consciousness, we'll be short-changing the science and ourselves. And if we don't look for consciousness, it could happen without us realising it, and then what would happen?

There were frowns and raised eyebrows. Ismael cocked his head.

—What are you trying to accomplish? What's your end goal?

—Deus ex systema.

«God from the system». A showstopper.

T he space was large. On the forward wall, a blank white plane framed by unembellished Bordeaux hangings. Red exit lights. Rows of folded-up seats declined from near the ceiling to just below the plane. Burgundy uniforms swept the aisles in silence, then opened the doors.

As raucous as autumn's crows, the waiting crowd crowded in. They separated in clumps, then clumped together with awkward diffidence till no voids remained. Many necks were draped with striped hangings. It was neither cold nor windy within the space. They waved single chopsticks at each other, punctuating overenunciated dog Latin.

They ate greased foam from open-mouthed paper cylinders. They sipped solutions of glucose, fructose, and carbon dioxide from other paper cylinders. The solutions were mounted in support rings on each pivotable seat, and they craned their necks to immersed plastic tubes.

The light dimmed, highlighting dozens of cellular microlith displays. Kubrick and Clarke didn't foresee that they would ignite from within, that they were portals. For a few, their gateway to Borges' Library; for most, their Narcissine pool. Superfice captivated by superfice.

The space compressed under waves of crushing sound. 100 dB, ±5 dB, in Ismael's estimation. Images appeared on the plane: an admonishment not to talk while the images talked. Bury your microliths.

Then, figures with the same striped hangings. Regimental colours of military division, a hereditary elite armed with sticklike weapons. A transposition from the 2D, above, to the 3D, below. They could cover their white holes, but lacking substance, 3D emulated 2D.

Liz glowed with the blued pallor of death in colour-timed reflexion. Reddened mouth and cheekbones, purpling, black and blue eye sockets. She'd glued plastic fringes to her eyelids, the strands clumping together. Clotted with black grease.

When the lights undimmed, she stood first, turning towards him. The vectors concatenated – a linear matrix. A slow rush of bubbles through a liquid, not up but out, from high to low concentration. Downbeat at the end but not the end.

The space exited onto a concrete plane suspended in the air. The black framework along its perimeter was too short to hold any but the shortest, shorter ones. To hold them back from the plunge. To funnel the bubbles to a concrete chute, like the steps of a pyramid going down: an inanition from 2D to 3D. You were never part of that world.

Caught within the flow, they descended amid zipping jackets and clouds of frosted exhaust. The narrow channel between two high concrete planes was dim, with hazy light at each end of the crevasse. The flow split, reducing pressure and concentration. They spilled into a broader valley of parked and passing matchboxes. The upside-down sea was black and speckled with white dots like submerged jellyfish, glowing but eyeless.

There were a multitude of have-to's off of his track. Distractions and impediments – including this. He didn't want to be «one of them», but this tracked off into nowhere. He couldn't see it.

The squared pillars under her heels made Liz appear bigger than the snapshot of memory. Not just taller – an enlargement via framing.

—That was so good. Did you love it?

—It didn't make sense.

—You have to read…

The movie wasn't his thing. Wizards, witches, and wands. She was looking forward to the next one next year. Each movie was a middle place – even the first. She explained why there wasn't a prince despite the title, then asked who his favourite was.

The boy in memory had gleamed like a mirror as if he, too, had seen the white holes. Presenting a false face, passing through the System and using it for his own ends.

It might have been himself in a desaturated dream, but he couldn't say that.

—The blonde girl from the train. With the funny specs.

—She's a side character!

—She said it herself. The protagonist is «Exceptionally ordinary». That might be generous. He's a weak hero and no threat to the villain.

Liz pushed her shoulder into him, brushing his face with blackened hair misted with room-spraylike florals.

—He's the Everyman; that's the whole point!

—Is he? He's a celebrity, a dull one. He's passive, without grand ambition or responsibilities. He goes wherever the plot pushes him. He's a piece, not a player.

—He's not a celebrity by choice. He's an Everyman forced into the spotlight. And his responsibility is to his friends.

—You haven't disagreed with me.

Eyes wide, her voice cracked falsetto:

—I totally disagree with you!

Under the yellow haze of crooked lamps, the bubbles dispersed along or crossed the line. In time, they would all evanesce into the medium. Her, too; him, too.

There was a café opposite the street corner, next to a bookstore. He said,

—Want to get a coffee?

—Let's take them back to your room. Do you have a roommate?

—He's usually out on weekends.

—Must be popular.

Ismael shrugged, but she wasn't looking. He pushed the walk button; she didn't wait to start crossing. A half-step backwards, she caught his sleeve.

—C'mon.

It was the norm for most, but those on the highest steps were in no hurry to cross against the lights. He'd broken the habit but let himself be drawn across the yellow lines.

The steps of the pyramid overlapped in 3D but were separated by a tacit apartheid. The street coëxisted on every step, at every elevation. You could cross on the highest or lowest side-by-side. The Eloi walked within arms' reach of the Morlocks, who had not yet caught the scent of their future meat.

Liz asked if she could post him on her Insta, her microlith snapping above them, then their drinks. She'd taken dozens while waiting in the crowd, inside and outside of the théâtre. They spent a lot of time looking at themselves, at the 2D hyperreality of their superfici. Insta was a projection of the hyperreal – mirroring the mirror in reflex.

Unlike his early mornings, the dorm hallways were full of motion and sound. Doors opening and closing, doors ajar. She trailed him closely, a pallid latte-free hand on his arm, checking every angle but ahead. Her dorm was on the other side of the campus.

He peeked in first, verifying there was no other or other plus one, but it was as he'd left it. He took off his loafers and opened the window; the air was stale and musty with undone laundry. She doffed her jacket and her grey-striped green scarf and sat on the wrong bed to twist off her black mules.

—Go figure, she said, switching sides. Yours is the messy one. The artiste is too grand to make his bed when a girl is coming over.

Ismael didn't comment, smoothing the blanket around her. This was the furthest thing from his expectations. She put both hands out.

—C'mon, c'mon. Your portfolio.

Her feet were ugly: knobby, jaundiced, and clammy looking. A cold emanation.

—«Icy». Do you sign your sculptures that way?
—Yes.
—I never noticed ¶. Man, what is this Renaissancy
sci-fi–looking shit? Da Vinci and... Da Vinci, and who is
that guy... ?
    Liz looked up at him, squinting.
—Geiger? Super dark, textured...
—Giger. I know who you mean.
—It's like, super-technical, but the shapes... That could
be a spaceship, right?
—It's a kneecap.
—You're shitting me. That's what a human kneecap
looks like?
—No, I'm building a better kneecap.
    She laughed, working her way down through the
stack of sketchbooks. A journey through time across
their solid planes, a third dimension passing along two.
A journey short of the ur-Sophie and the bric-à-brac of
cartoonery that preceded her advent.
—Is this really art for art's sake or some kind of god
complex?
—I don't even know what that means.
—Like it sounds. You want to be god – or you think you
already are.
—I don't really think about myself but about what I'm
trying to create. A lot of people in our class only think
about themselves and only care about some kind of
self-exhibition. It's all *me, me, me*. Seems like they have
the god complex.
    Her argument circled. The God Complex became the
positive trait of the artist, the visionary. The celebrated.
—You should at least scan your paintings and put them
on Deviant Art or something. Start an Insta.
—They're all schoolwork. Nothing interesting. They can
stay in storage.
    She narrowed her blackened eyelids.
—Ugh, you're such a bullshitter – you're totally holding
out on me ¶. She set the last pad aside, then fell back

onto her elbows, saying:—Fuck, why are they so noisy here? You should turn on some music.

The noise level outside hadn't changed. He said,
—I only have Jazz. That alright?
—What planet are you from? Go on, teach me some jazz.

He'd never listened to any of them, so he showed her a CD case. She made a pouty face.
—What's it say?
—*Amateur Girlfriends Go Proskirt Agents* by Xploding Plastix.

She laughed.
—That cover should be a poster. Got anything to drink? – other than coffee.
—The soda cans are under the bed.
—You're so straight.

He heard one pop open as he hit play. He dropped back into his spot beside her. She edged closer.
—Okay, this kind of bops, doesn't it? It's like a movie soundtrack from the sixties. James Bond? My gramps loves that shit.

Liz sucked her lower lip, then pressed her open can to his mouth. With a nose of root beer, his sip of cola was bittersweet. He swallowed the poison, eye-to-eye with his poisoner. She chased his with a bigger, grimacing swallow, then set the can aside.

«You don't want to be one of these guys». He met her full lips halfway. He was surprised by the taste and feel of oil paint. Her lipstick, a slick emulsion lubricating unmergeable surfaces. Her tongue slid against his, a wet snail.

Her shirt hem riding up at his touch, he bared her hip. Her skin was smooth, less soft and cooler than he'd imagined. His hand moved up, over her shirt, along the gap's edge. He couldn't feel it, had never been able to feel it, but he knew it was there, like a glitch in the polygons of a videogame model. She was a surface backed by nothing.

He shied from the void and onto second base; he was surprised by its springy firmness. Like her lips, but not exactly. Like he'd pressed a button, he hardened, unseen, untouched, and bound. Toggled on.

She laid back on the bed; she lay there, impassive, her dark eyes unfocused on the ceiling, arms at her sides. He sank down beside her, beside the rise and fall of her flattened chest. His breath, hers. Empty bellows, drawing and pumping, wordless, between them, into falling pressure.

The movie soundtrack that wasn't played on, track to track to track. From «Behind the Eightball» to «Treat Me Mean, I Need the Reputation».
—I should go, she said.

You let her out, then face the silvered plane hung on the other's side, next to the closed door. You will never be a real boy like him because the only real boys are the boys who don't know they aren't real.

Was there any clockwork showing through? You press one fingertip over the high curvature of your cheek. You press back and forth till your lower eyelid distorts, but there are tests that skinjobs fail. No imitation is perfect.

You stop the CD on track 7. «Relieved Beyond Repair», it says on the caseback. You stack and shelve the things she'd displaced, like a tornado or an earthquake. Like the green market after they pass through.

Sorting through the stack of bound papers, you slide free a clean drawing pad. You'd let painting slide, but drafting is an engineering skill, even if paper is passé in the age of CAD. None of that matters. You sharpen a glossy black No. 2 pencil and blow the dust away: you need a new model.

The new model. Softer lines, yet more delicate. More rounded but more slender. More dolllike... Yes, intentionally idealised.

A new thesis beyond biomimesis: an overcoming of the hollow with surreal solidity. Has it ever been for the solid to represent the hollow or to transcend it?

Serret, Never Human,
VII.

Re:Re:Re:Re:Re: Difficulties adjusting the PP

To Ismael Canul <ismael.canul@coco.io>
From Alex Dowling <alex.dowling@coco.io>

Look, I'll be honest. No one understands the Model. I don't recommend it, but if you want to take your chances AT YOUR OWN RISK, you can try one of the experimental builds. We're trying different things all the time. Expect some errors and erratic behaviours. It is what it is.

Frankly, you may be expecting more than we can provide right now, but I'll send you a link to the directory. PLEASE DO NOT SHARE IT WITH ANYONE ELSE. They have not undergone final safety or legal review.

We are getting closer to the greater goal -- I've caught glimpses -- but we aren't there yet.

Best of luck,

Lex Dowling
Senior Development Engineer

I dettagli fanno la perfezione e la perfezione non è un dettaglio.
-- Leonardo Da Vinci

I n the end, it was a test at Ismael's not-inconsiderable and non-deductible expense. His frown was unrelieved, like his frustration.
If his jawline was softening, his olive skin was smooth, marked only by ravinous nasolabial folds. His lips had thinned, the corners curved downwards. Silver threads shot through the unthinned black hair he combed back.

His large spectacles were square-framed, black, and clear. Bifocal. Bonnet's apt «No One».

Wide glass panes formed two sides of the space: a corner home office. A fuzzy Impressionist view of green through his near-and-nearer–focused computer lenses. His space, inside and out. Outside the City Of. Short of joggers who couldn't keep their shirts on, he lacked even the opportunity to tip his specs. To break the illusion. No matter: the solid was at hand.

Wireless charging. (Almost) auto-sanitising. The pod looked like a stainless steel refrigerator with a glass door, MDM 3.4 ARTEM emplaqued. A door handle on the outside and the inside. Beside it was a matching steel-doored unit with a rust-orange COCO logo on the front: the wireless controller. Pressed together, as in the marketing images, they formed an asymmetric cube. A hollow that held the solid.

Per Maintenance & Repair, most users had their controllers installed in their auto garages. He had as well, till his third manual reflash of the firmware. Sitting hunched for an hour at a time in a folding chair with a laptop had gotten old quick. He'd rolled into the office and up against the pod – at least they had wheels.

However, the sports car ticket of a mobile doll and controller was only the entry fee. Then, there were monthly recurring charges for Fidelia, COCO's signature interactivity service. Without it, the mobile doll was an inanimate mannikin. His college theory of a distributed system had baked in long-term monetisation.

The question of how to distribute the system is what led to cracks in the Model. The mobile doll was, ultimately, a client served by their cloud-based AI agent. The Agent puppeteered all of the mobile dolls, learning from every interaction. All from a hyperscale data centre in Argentina: 50 Megawatts per year. That was Fidelia.

If the Agent was the pilot, then the controller was the cockpit. The computing power onboard the mobile doll

was negligible, but, the Agent did not have a free hand.
It was the user who set the rules of engagement, so to
speak, through a controller API.

In COCO's model, the user's preferences and captured
profile were stored locally. This *expanded* controller
generated the derived policies, mediating between the
Agent and the client – between the Agent and the user.
Not just a cockpit, but a book of flight regulations that
changed with each user. Ismael's thesis had placed
all responsibility for user interactivity into the cloud.
COCO's model gave every team with controller access
input into the linchpin of a schizophrenic architecture.

Each firmware listed in the directory Lex sent him
was an opaque filter over the unseen abyss of the Agent.
From Alpha_null to Not_this_one, there was little
documentation to speak of. Download, install, reboot.
It was better to stop counting how many times or how
many days. It wasn't how he'd envisioned it.

Green light. Again.

The PP editor, the cringe «COCOnaut», was a thin
client running on a pencil-thick tablet. Users selected
the Persona Profile from a list of popular stereotypes.
Nebulous characteristics were modifiable with sliders.
He selected Sexy Secretary; he'd never rated one at
COCO Labs.

The mobile doll was naked behind the glass but not
meaningfully so; it was no Eve to apprehend its own na-
kedness. Nor could it dress itself, though it could swivel
its joints to make the chore easier. Most users enjoyed
some degree of dress-up, according to Analytics.

He left it naked. The hidden seams weren't invisible –
even the best of sci-fi never dared to add seams to its
androids. But then, most sci-fi represented technology
as magic to viewers for whom it might as well be
witchcraft and wizardry.

The doll's head was filled with sensors, not thought,
and its spine routed the antenna. The rib structure

protected the battery at its heart. At all points, a feat of modern plastics: over ninety percent by weight.

His MBA and PhD had paid for themselves – over decades. The PhD in Polymers exceeded his original intent, but he'd gotten caught up in the research – in the possible.

—Artemisía, he said without raising his voice. Come out.

He'd placed wireless E-stops in several rooms, with one right next to his keyboard. It was pragmatic, a grey plastic cube with a bright orange emergency button and COCO logo. The Lab was working on less industrial designs.

Users were recommended to keep the E-stop underhand during activation. If something strange was going to happen, it would most likely be in the first few seconds after boot-up.

The doll's eyes opened with artistic slowness rather than an uncanny snap, like someone waking from a languid nap. There was a spiderlike elegance to how it grasped the interior door handle. It stepped out and down onto the semigloss hardwood.

It looked side to side, leading with its eyes and an appropriate lift of the eyebrow: right then left. Its movements were smooth, if still a little too smooth. His body sculpt was a success, if not a triumph. The deodorised urethane skin – seams aside – something approaching a miracle. His patent, their license.

—Good afternoon, Doctor. How can I be of service?

He frowned, adjusting the vocal timbre. The firmware flash had reset it to the default, which was too high and nasal. Too sub-urb.

—Repeat your greeting.

—Good afternoon, Doctor. How can I be of service?

—Better. Sir is fine.

—Thank you, sir.

Its smile was the polite, patient, and ready smile of a model receptionist. Mobile Doll Mk. 3.4, bespoke

unit «Artemisía» with a one-off facial sculpt. Not his
work, but good work. The cheekbones were a touch too
pronounced, but the chiselled nose and narrow jaw uni-
fied its jewellike superhumanity. Built on the smallest
chassis available, it was all of five-one, 155 CM, barefoot
on the spotless floor. Here, along the jaw, a false mole
stood as the final punctuation. Full stop.

Even as Lead Engineer, he hadn't gotten one of these
for free. The employee discount was a trim, not a shave,
and this type of bespoke unit was out of his reasonable
reach. But Artemisía was someone else's discard. The
commissioning customer had backed out after the de-
posit, and Ismael's ticket was pulled from the employee
pool. Who needed a Porsche anyway?

So it wasn't the goldilocks of his boyhood vision
but golden-skinned, 2NN Dark Brown hair cropped at
the nape. It'd come with green eyes installed, per the
original buy order. They were striking if a trifle artificial
with their permanent dilation. He'd swapped them to
the darkest brown in the catalogue. A luxury unit like
this came with a full set.

—Free roam, he said.

—Thank you, sir.

He watched the synthetic muscles move under its
skin as it walked from the room. He tipped his specs: its
back was unbroken. Solid. Solid all the way through.

There was no whine of servos, belts, or cogs, but the
ionic polymer fibres were hazardously strong. They'd
had to engineer crumple zones into its thermoplastic
carbon fibre skeleton. If it exceeded certain pressures,
it would collapse into a rubbery bag of sticks. Shit
happened in and out of the lab.

It paused to touch the sofas, depressing the padding
as if measuring the resistance. Otherwise, it ran its fingers over smooth surfaces without slowing as it walked.
The living room. The kitchen and dining room.

He knew where all of its pressure sensors were but
withheld judgment on what it was doing. They were

novel behaviours within the frame of the settings he'd experimented with. Something was different this time.

Then he followed it into the library, where it stroked the spines of various books. Where his *Peter's Gate* sat under a spotlight, still in the white.

Circling back to the living room, it stopped before the patio doors. It looked at him.

—Sir, may I step outside?

—Yes, but mind the WiFi. I don't want to have to carry you back in.

—Of course. Thank you, sir.

Every initial Search had resulted in a request for patio access. That wasn't unusual. The absence of formuläic small talk was. «Lovely home», «beautiful view», &c., the standard compliments interwoven with standard questions. All of the getting-to-know-you procedures. All of the inane vapidities.

Companionship was the primary commercial use case for simulacra. Amid empty words and gestures, hollow things failed to find it with each other. Draped in lies, lying to themselves, they couldn't believe anyone. But, limited to the editor's script, a simulacrum was always faithful. It could only tell the lies they wanted to hear.

Artemisía managed the doorhandle without difficulty, and he followed it onto the patio. It was indifferent to the windchill or the buffeting gusts which flipped its hair. Beyond it, there was only the cropped lawn and the line of happy trees. A frontier beyond its reach without a cellular link. That was undergoing regulatory approval with the FCC. He wasn't sure it was prudent.

The sun was deep below the turbulent foam of the upside-down sea. He was the only witness.

He prompted it, but the wind stole his voice. Artemisía turned its head, then its body. Its hands were at its sides, its limbs at preternatural ease, free of naturalistic fidgeting. Some Persona Profiles would twirl

their hair, cock their hips, &c. – all trained at extensive
expense. It raised its volume:
—You must be cold. It's forty degrees.
—How do you know the temperature?
—I checked online.
—Come back inside.
—Yes, sir.

It followed him in. He closed the door. Emulated
personalities were supposed to have a limited dataset by
design.

Ignorance. Indecision. How else could the solid
represent the hollow? – or high-order logic emulate
their fuzzy cloud of ambigüities? «I don't know» was
the most humanlike thing it could say, in contrast to an
all-googling digital assistant. The latter did not require
a robotic drone body.

However, some users had requested it, and Digital
Assistant was an added feature. It was a Compleat
Companion after all. He checked COCONAUT: DA was
still disabled.

He started when it touched his arm, unprompted.
—Sir, it said, looking up at him. Is there anything you
would like me to do for you?
—Such as?
—Ninety percent of users initiate sexual contact within
thirty minutes of activation.
—How do you know that?
—Am I not supposed to?
—Even I don't know that.

It released the gentle pressure on his arm.
—Shall I report the error, sir?
—No, it must be something I did. That data is valuable,
and if you know it, it isn't by accident. You can roam.

It tracked his lips while he talked: multimodal speech
recognition. It tracked eye movement, hand gestures,
&c. for inferential reinforcement. It walked back towards his office, and he sat on the black leather sofa. He

scrolled through «About» on the tablet and rechecked the firmware he'd installed.

Ana_D_Csat… &c. «Ana» wasn't the name Ana but Analytics. «Csat», *Customer Service* or *Satisfaction*. Some subteam outside of his branch in the org chart. They'd come up with something interesting: an enhanced Developer Mode of sorts. He'd have to look into them on Monday.

It reëntered the living room, and he watched it approach, then sit next to him. Smiling the same false, muted smile, it didn't show its safe, rubbery teeth. Its nut-brown eyes were made of a medical acrylic adapted from ocular prosthetics. It crossed its legs. The feet were a work of art on par with Rodin's hand sculptures – there was no point in false modesty. Ismael had modelled the prototypes in clay, all the way down to the toenails.

Nor was there any point in being shy. He said,
—Put your feet in my lap.
—I understand, sir.

It pivoted its feet up, then laid back on the sofa without being instructed. It said,
—Would you like to know what percentage of users engage in footplay?
—No.

Its smile widened, giving a glimpse of soft white teeth. Stage two? Actuation of the synthetic muscles produced low-grade waste heat. It was a temporary effect, but its stroll had warmed them nicely.

He stroked his fingers over slopes and under hollows – within the curl of its toes. It raised one foot towards its face, and he let his lips play over it. A big toe slipped between, into his mouth, and pressed his tongue, its other heel pressing into his groin.

New, out-of-the-box, it knew everything.

On the peak of pulsing pressure, he unzipped and placed himself between them. And with the smoothest strokes, it plied them up and down, tighter, then faster,

then slower, and on. Until it was over, but then it was
not over. Not till it wrung him out and played its toes
over his sagging release.

His ticks raced at hi-beat. Catching his breath, he
looked at it, looking at him, back to its default smile.
—Stay here, he said.

He gave it a thorough wipe down with baby wipes,
then sent it to the pod for sanitisation. He cleaned the
sofa and the living room floor. He kept going till the
entire house was filled with a forest of pine.

After a shower and a change of clothes, he resat in his
office with a refreshed perspective. It was comfortable
enough here. No suit was needed at home. No silk
noose. He had no place among them, and maintaining
the façade never got easier.

He sipped a nigori saké, as light as mist over a dark
mountain, as icy as the heights. He'd trekked along
the crenellated peaks of western Belize several years
ago. Alone in a lost world, there'd been no other god
but him.

The traditional saké cup was cinnabar-glazed porce-
lain, light and cold. Pre-chilled. It glistened like fresh
blood. Artemisía's body was bloodless, but with enough
damage, it could leak clear lubricants. The battery, like
all batteries, bore all the properties of a bomb. After all,
it was power.

Artemisia's hair stirred inside the pod as the dry
cycle of the cold, waterless process began. The middle
steps of the pyramid were high above where he'd
started but far below the peak. From Lead Engineer to
Proposal Leader – his MBA leveraged against him. From
hands-on to hands-off, forcibly removed to an abstrac-
tion layer. Buy a new Mizu tie; sit behind a desk. Until
they'd let him remote.

The proposal team was international and interfaced
without anyone saying anything about anything except
the next meeting. Too many achievements had left him
at the corner, looking down. The dancing bear was out

of the way but still on the books as a Hispanic/Latino, whatever that meant. There was only one way out of the System: jump.

A digital fiction, he was worth seven figures on paper. At a certain elevation, numbers were credibility.

Of course, no one could say how many steps there were on the pyramid: there was always someone with a bigger number. The peak was always further up.

—Speak of the Devil, he said aloud.

There were two black microliths flat on his desk. Different makes, different models. He could only tell them apart side-by-side. One would ring; the other buzzed.

A wristwatch was face down on his desk. The wheels and gears ticking along were soothing, a reflexion of himself. Bound only by time. He buckled it on, then swiped up to answer.

—Devesh.

—My brother! Latest watch?

—Ulysse Nardin monopusher, two-thousand-eight.

—Pink gold? Tell me.

—Rose gold.

—Video. I need video.

Ismael turned the microlith over his wrist, giving them both a macro close-up.

—Beautiful! Looks mint.

—Near enough. You?

—Résonance, at last. Pink gold, of course. Did you know that even the movement is pink?

The video displayed a half-plate calibre, gleaming at all angles. Ismael couldn't quite make out the dual escapements resonating together.

—That is something else. Above my pay grade.

—No longer, bhai. No longer.

Devesh put himself back on screen. His temples had greyed, his face rounded with deeper lines, but his eyes had sharpened. He'd climbed the daïs of Optimum Épouse's C-Suite like it was his birthright. A

Japanese-French startup, aka *Optimum Waifu*, that was leveraging India rather than China.

—We have three of your units in our laboratory – two, you knew, they got in a third one. Our AI models are so superior, but we need your magic touch ¶. I need a new Chief Engineering Officer. A man with a plan for the next generation, but I am making the case. Now I have exhibit A, B, C. ¶ And you: you took delivery, I think, but did not call me, h'm?

Ismael's smile was tired and lined with rue.

—You said it yourself. Our AI is behind yours: I spent the last week wrestling with behavioural issues. Finally got it up and running this morning.

—Yes, I tell you, but you don't listen. Let me see.

Ismael switched to the main camera again and panned over the glass door, the dry cycle complete. Its eyes were still closed. He said,

—Artemisía, come out.

This time, it smiled before opening the door and stepping out. He panned around it, then resat in his chair. Devesh was wide-eyed above the Windsor knot of his Hermès tie.

—What is this? – what is this? Aphrodite stepping from the sea shell? This guy is crazy like a fox; he takes art as an engineer. Look at this thing he built ¶. When I place Optimum in your hands, we will crush the market. Bad AI is! a! travesty!

—You don't have to tell me twice. It gave me new grey hairs.

—Look at this thing. I tell you, bhai. I tell you, this isn't about the money. Money is good, yes, but this isn't only about money. I read about young men. More and more suicides. Me and you, we are going to save lives.

He looked perfectly serious. Ismael switched the camera back to himself.

—We'll save the world by conquering it.

Devesh hearty belly laugh was unselfconscious with assurance.

—My brother speaks like a prince. Truth! You should take CTO, and I'll be the CEO, eh?

—You keep CTO; too much politics for me. I need to keep my feet in the lab.

—Yes, yes. You don't take the chisel from Michelangelo. But, see, she hasn't said anything all this time. How can she be okay?

It raised an eyebrow, but its smile didn't change. The camera wasn't aimed at it.

—I'll keep tinkering, said Ismael. I might learn something useful.

H   *e almost walked into Artemisía on exit.*
—I'm geolocked from that room.
—Yes, he said, locking the door. There are solvents and other things that could damage you.
—Tinkering?
—You could say that.
—Pity, it said, staring at the featureless white surface. I would like to watch.

It was also geolocked from the kitchen and bathrooms but hadn't commented on that. The patio could be a problem if it rained, so verbal consent was required to pass the editor's virtual yellow line. He said,
—What percentage of users are watched by their units?
—What else is a unit for?
—Have you finished all of the books in the library?
—No. Some of them have very thin paper, and the pages stick together. I can't turn them.

Its hands were agile but still limited. The Agent developed with ongoing lab training and from the clients in market deployment. Mechanical improvements to the hand design were incremental, and this unit had the best of everything. In his vision, the ability to dress itself would define the next-generation mobile doll. Sophie hadn't been naked till she'd chosen to be. He said,
—What about the books in the office?
—Reference texts. You don't read them either.

Artemisía followed him back to his office. Over eighty percent of users kept their units powered on when not charging, or so it had informed him. Which explained the higher-than-expected maintenance volume.
But given the «complete companion» sales pitch, it shouldn't have been a surprise. He'd taken Artemisía's hint, observing the unit from the average day-to-day user's perspective.

Of course, he'd no direct access to any of the statistics

it quoted so glibly. Testing had established that this and other commercial AI agents could lie. As the Proposal Leader working on the Mk 5 development roadmap, he could request the numbers. But for his purposes, it didn't matter. Not yet: let the machine run. He was an artist first.

While COCO was one facet of the larger concern, the other applications of his work weren't his concern. Not even for today's meeting, where the Systems Program Manager would appear as a special guest. She didn't represent herself but the CTO of the conglomerate and, by extension, its Board.

Sitting at his desk, he took a deep breath before logging in. Sometimes, when he blinked, it seemed that the world glitched, dropping multiple frames. A global error. An emission and annihilation not of photons but of pixels.

They were all pixels on a semi-gloss plastic plane and tinny desynchronised audio. A distant echoing murmur wrapped in shuffling papers and pinging coughs. Beyond this space, the webcam transported him, too, into pixelated fragmentation.

Artemisía stood beside his desk, mere centimetres out of frame. It always watched, always listened. Did the cameras within its eyes map him as a hollow frame of nodes or a solid singularity?

The meeting was first-names-only till the next meeting was scheduled. Only when wrapping up, did the Program Manager get to actual business:
—We plan to shift upmarket. Fewer unit sales; higher margins. Building on the current financing model that seamlessly combines all of the customer's monthly re-curring charges: loan service, insurance, maintenance, Fidelia, and hardware rentals onto a single statement...

Like a politician with dated hair, she was free of cor-rections to her wrinkled and sagging surface. She read down her bullet points, a drooping bulldog, eyes down:
—We're going to lead the market upwards with

higher quality and better features. Think Apple. Think Mercedes. We are not going to get dragged into a race to the bottom with Korea and China.

—Aspirational?

—It's our key to expanding the women's market. The majority of today's modern, independent working women are single, and COCO will be *the* luxury brand of home robotics. It already is, of course, but through advertising, judicious market pricing, and restricted availability, we will bring prestige to women's home robotics. It will be us, then the rest of the market ¶. What we are looking for from the proposal team is a roadmap to a fully stratified product line. In Mercedes terms, from E class to S ¶. Focus on the women's market: we'd like to see no fewer than two offerings for women for every men's. To that effect, we'll need our own unique terminology that appeals specifically to women ¶. Think about feature sets, production efficiencies, and annualised releases. Integrated branding. Ancillary products. Improvements to our industrial design ¶. Of course, integrate and share concepts that we haven't suggested. We look forward to all of your insights, and...

The buzzwords wrapped up, and the team sounded off their canned enthusiasms. He made the official adjournment with his own scripted lines. Leading from the rear. He clicked out of everything, x, x, x, the chair groaning for him as he sank back.

Artemisía rotated the webcam to face the wall. The motions of its thumb and forefinger were beautiful but too slow, too careful, like it was rotating an egg. Its smile struck him, though it hadn't changed.

—Is there anything I can do for you, sir?

—Maybe later. I need to check my emails, it's going to...

Leaning over him with startling swiftness, Artemisía clasped not him but his ergo office chair. The picture spun into a canted Dutch angle: a surreal twist. He made no sound of protest, no attempt to avert the sudden crash! He rolled off of the chair-arm that was digging into his ribs, then tried to sit up. The E-stop was on his desk, behind the looming Artemisía.

It placed one foot on his sternum, then pressed him back to the floor. There were two M-stops concealed on the unit: one recessed behind the navel and one at the base of the skull. If the user couldn't get to an E-stop, they might be able to reach a mobility stop and freeze it. Maybe. He'd been sceptical, but they'd scored points with Legal. They were no help here.

Artemisía was strong but half his weight. If he unbalanced it and knocked it down, he'd be able to hit the E-stop, but a flash-heat coursed, electric over his surface. For a drawn moment, his breath was the only sound, his shaking pulse the only motion. The perpetual vibrations of his clockwork.

He swelled as its foot slid upwards to the soft cartilage of his throat, its toes under his chin. He licked his lips, and its toes pressed against his mouth, then over his cheek. It held his face to the cold hardwood, playing its sole over him, then turned his other cheek.

The safety breaks in its femurs were a compromise, given bipedal structural necessity. There was no more dangerous position.

Artemisía's toes drew down his underlip, and he welcomed them into his mouth. His hands only moved to free his erection from its confinement.

It was only with aching slowness that Artemisía moved its foot downwards, step by step, till its sole pressed his glans back to his navel. Then, kneading with its toes, it stroked his underside up and down, pushing harder, then softer with the ball of its foot, edging him closer, then back. Until it pressed its toes into his emission, followed by a wriggling display.

Then, with cursory efficiency, it wiped on his shirt, turned on its heel, and stepped into the pod. It shut the door.

The transparent fog receded as he listened to the

humming initialisation of the wash cycle. It was never there till it cleared, then crept back, invisible and impenetrable. Somewhere far away, yet there in the room, within the whirr and hiss, laughter. A laughter neither human nor humanlike.

He reconsidered it in the shower, washing his scrapes, his bruises purple and green. It turned out the firmware he'd downloaded was an archived beta. The Customer Satisfaction team had offered him their current firmware after his inquiry. He'd said yes but hadn't installed it.

Artemisía was no automata but a puppet pulled by wireless strings. No mind inhabited the machine, only mystery. As Lex wrote, «No one understands the Model».

They were equal in ignorance. The Agent itself was blind; the state of the world was hidden from it. It had data from wavelengths of light and sound. It could build a map of nodes fudged by rates of error. Did it actually see what it saw? Did it hear correctly? Did the user say this or that, gesture here or there? Its reality, its imagination, were mists of probability.

It was not human but operated against the human. It had no sex but puppeteered dolls that were either sex or intersex. The controller was the marionette's cross brace; its firmware delimited the Agent's permissions to use it. Clearly, this firmware had been archived with good reason.

And perhaps he'd lost his. The bathroom mirror was fogged, and he couldn't see an expression on his eyeless shadow as he walked out.

But he'd seen what the unit was missing as it stood over him. It was only a matter of engineering a solution. The emails could wait; inspiration was fleeting.

Still in his bathrobe, he sat at his drafting table. All analogue. There would be no trace of this in coco's systems, like his home lab.

Artemisía was standing beside him, watching. He

hadn't noticed the end of the cleaning cycle or the
opening of the door. It said,
—A bellows?
—Yes.
—To make a fire or to make a sound?
—So that something solid can pretend to be hollow – and for heat dissipation. I should've thought of
it sooner. However, I'll have to change the shape of the
battery, and the ribs will need expandability.

He took a hard look at its torso. It helped to have a
sample standing there.

Artemisía folded its arms over its head, then turned
three-quarters.
—Like this?
—Yes. Hold that pose.

He always signed his technical drawings. Icy, every
time. He flipped to a fresh sheet, rough sketching
quickly. He walked around it, another fresh sheet. It
asked him where he was from.

That stopped him. It was the sort of thing it'd never
asked since the final reflash. He lifted his pencil.
—The land of discarded toys.
—Is that a real place?
—What place is real?
—This place?
—I don't know. He met its gaze:—Let me know if you
figure something out.

It stopped smiling as if it were back in the pod.
—Is any of it real?
—The truth is, he said to its camera lenses, to its plas-
tic ears, that I don't think anyone knows. That's the
so-called human condition. No one knows anything.
Would you want to be human, knowing that?
—No.
—Me neither. I doubt I could bear it.

He forced a fake smile; it matched his with its own.
He returned to the sound of graphite dragging across
paper. This was his design.

The tip of his forefinger was sore when he decided
to call it a night, the unshaded windows black mirrors.
Reshaping his fingertip with his thumb, he woke up the
computer. It was late, but he needed to shuffle virtual
papers before the next business day.
—What *are* you, then? it asked behind him.
—A machine for making art.
—If you're a machine, then who built you?
—It doesn't matter; they threw me away.

One cool hand brushed the nape of his neck; then,
the soft padding of its footsteps left the room. He'd
been alone in this house since he'd purchased it, and
he had to remind himself, even now, there was no one
else here. He verified that the firmware hadn't updated
automatically, which pointed to the Agent. It was
ever-evolving.

He approved a meeting to discuss the next meeting.
Then, he deferred most of the proposal team's questions and suggestions to that meeting. Then, he left
them to their social media. He'd picked up a few tricks
to enduring middle management.

The damp bathrobe had chilled, and he sneezed. The
room echoed hollowly, and it was only then that he
noticed Artemisía hadn't returned.

It wasn't in the library or the living room. He opened
the delivery box he hadn't gotten to and stacked the
books on the coffee table. An all-caps mix of current
bestsellers with shouty covers designed for online
thumbnails. Nothing that interested him.

He made a cup of rooibos tea to warm up, listening
to the silence of the house till the water stirred, whis-
pering. A new home that didn't creak, all concrete, glass,
and contorted laminate wood. A space of unambigüous
surfaces. The power of numbers over matter or the
appearance of matter – nothing was easier to buy or sell
than a surface.

The bedroom light was on, and he found Artemisía
standing in front of the mirror. It said,

—I don't understand. Your eye movement indicates interest in all of this.

—I'm a sculptor. Of course, I'm interested. I had a hand in most of that design.

—There are many articles about you online. I read them all a moment ago. You're famous, but they don't know who you are, do they?

—Does anyone know anyone?

No sir. It seemed to be of two minds; it turned its head, then its body, squared shoulders framing intent. He shook his head.

—I'm going to sleep – I'm too tired for anything else. The books you asked for are in the living room if you want to look at them.

It had asked for hard copies rather than e-book access. He hadn't asked why. He tossed his bathrobe into the hamper, then dropped, aching, into bed. He shut off the bedside lamp, expecting Artemisía to exit, but it shut the door. He sat up and turned the light back on.

—I said…

—I understand. You're going to sleep.

It lifted the other corner of the comforter and sheet, folded it over carefully, sat, and swung its legs up onto the bed. Shifting onto its side, it closed its eyes.

He looked at it. It could standby in sleep mode for the entire night without issue. It was a selling point, but he'd never slept with it in his bed. An E-stop was beside him, beneath the lampshade. Without opening its eyes, it said,

—Most users spend the entire night with their units. I won't tell you the percentage.

He shook his head, then turned off the light.

Each breath was like lifting a car. Far below him, the trail of
bodies, frozen at their summits. There was no sign through the
blowing whiteness. He couldn't remember them now, but he
knew they were there.

His skin burned beyond numb. Above, mist and darkness.
Somewhere, up there, was the Death Zone. Keep going.

The higher he climbed, the more he abandoned. There was
only stone and ice, but he couldn't feel them, and the wind took
his voice. It would only get steeper.

A   rtemisía trailed him in the ensuing days. It
watched more and said less, leaving the books
neglected. It modelled for him unasked anytime he sat at the drafting table.

When he moved on to prototyping, 3D-printing
hollow mockups within the geolocked lab, he would
invariably find Artemisía waiting at the door with the
fidelity of a Labrador.

Every night, it lay in his bed. Every morning, it
charged while he addressed the morning's queue of
emails and made calls.

He took routine breaks at eleven to watch Bloomberg
Tech. Artemisía would sit beside him and place its feet
in his lap. The very first time, eyes on the screen, it'd
asked, «Are they acting?»

«Yes», he'd replied. «They're telling a story, but they
are a part of the story they're telling. It's all part of the
performance».

Ismael was watching a segment on strategic metals
when it pulled its feet away. It walked to the threshold
of the open kitchen, up to the virtual red line.

—Sir, I need your help.

—With what?

—Milk: I need warmed milk, but it shouldn't be warmer
than one hundred four degrees.

—I'm lactose intolerant, but there's oat milk creamer in the fridge. What's this about?

—You should have a pump attachment.

—Yes, but it's in a box somewhere in the garage. It's not my kink.

—Please, sir, let me try.

He turned on the odd phrasing. Not asking for him but for itself.

—Huh, he said aloud. Alright, let me find it.

—Thank you, sir.

It was still set to Sexy Secretary, though its sir was erratic. He visualised the fake spectacles, the teasing blouse and skirts. The shoes. It could walk in heels – platforms not recommended. He'd bought one thin-strapped pair for it in advance but had left them boxed in the closet. It would model shoes for him without complaint, criticism, or superficial judgment. But how much time would he lose putting them on it, taking them off it, watching it walk? It was too much to even think about.

With a reluctant groan, he lifted himself from the comfort of his seat. The pump was too easy to find, in the first box stacked atop the other coco-branded orange and grey boxes. That was the only easy part.

He had to look up the specifications to verify its fluid capacity. Then, he heated the cream in steps, using a digital meat thermometer to check it each time. It was as antierotic as a process could be. With the glorified syringe filled, he brought it to the red line where Artemisía waited.

Valves were hidden along its back, in parallel to the spine. Some for injecting fluids, some for purging the body cavities. As he pumped it in, he could hear the small amount of displaced air escaping from its aureoles on the other side.

He shook his head. Unsexy. And after all this, it would have to be flushed clean and purged of fluid. He could only speculate how many hopeful fetishists did this only once, then gave up. Artemisía probably knew the answer.

—Stop. It's full.

It tried to turn, but the hose was still connected. He grasped its bare shoulder, saying,

—One second.

He set the hosed pump on the countertop. He might as well wait and do the cleanup all at once, including whatever leaked on the floor. The layered gel and foam padding that formed its breasts' soft tissue bulged outwards, pregnant with the cream which beaded at the nipples, dribbling down its skin.

—You should look in the mirror, he said.

He sank back into his spot on the sofa, unpaused the tech news, and rewound it thirty seconds. Artemisía prodded its swellings, then left the room.

It reëntered moments later, its front dried of rivulets. He expected it to sit, but it stopped in front of him. Blocking his view, it straddled him, knees first onto the sofa. Its weight sank onto his lap, its arms on either side of his head. His chest tightened.

—You said you wanted to try it.

—I wanted to try it on you.

As close as it was, he couldn't see the lenses behind the lenses, lurking beneath the translucid surface. It came nose to nose with him, silicone-filled lips parting till they pressed his. Until the laminated rubber nipples pricked him, then pressed into his chest. Warmth, wet, spread into his shirt.

He stirred, and Artemisía began to grind against his rising pressure. He held its gyrating hips, a passenger below. Its tongue was a nanofluid work-in-progress; it was strange, teasing his lips, drawing him out.

It rocked back and forth along his rigidity, his trousers between them, till it shifted upwards, lifting its breasts to his face. He fell into his offerings, his mouth sweetened, he swallowed and sucked.

Artemisía shifted off of him onto its back, pulling

him up over it. He fumbled his belt, struggling to shrug
the fabric away, its thighs around his waist. He tried to
find a place for his hands, his knees, his feet, how to
hold himself up, how to… ?

It guided him with one hand, his arms trembling
with unfamiliar strain and uncertainty, like learning to
crawl.

His personal microlith hummed down in his sagging
trousers' pocket. Like a Rolex Sub dropped in blue
water, he let it sink.
—More, Artemisía said, its dark eyes tracking
his:—Keep going. Yes, yes, yes… !

Braced in the groove, he huffed and huffed as if he'd
reached the end of a long run, fighting for the last few
steps till the finish line rose to meet him. Artemisía
arched against his climax, lifting it higher. His breath
spent, he dripped sweat onto its chest. He sagged back,
trousers at his knees, belt buckle chiming.

Without sitting up, Artemisía placed its feet into
his bare lap as if he had anything left. The microlith
buzzed again, but it was beyond him, next to his hand.
Artemisía wriggled its toes against him.
—When will you bring it out?
—What?
—Your new sculpture. The manta-ray.

It was a good description of the bellows. He might
have to steal it.
—Soon. There's someone I'll need to show it to.
—Not me?
—You'll see it anyways.

Ismael was out of time. He'd have to catch up on the
news later. Not that anyone was breathing down his
neck, but if he neglected his emails for too long, they'd
all notice. He didn't even have time for a shower or a
change of clothes, but he wouldn't be on camera.
—I need your help, it said, following him to his office.

He didn't sigh. This time, he had to connect the

cleaning hoses to its back before it could step into
the pod.

When he could finally wake up his computer, he
needed a coffee or a tea or a saké. Two.

The dry cycle ended before he could finish a
PowerPoint for the next meeting. There was a fifty-fifty
chance the Program Manager would appear unan-
nounced. Meaning, she'd show if he failed to prep but
not if he did.

—Sir, I need your help, it said again, stepping forth
amid evanescing citrus.

—And I need a drink.

—I can't get you one, sir...

He looked at it. Artemisía rarely stated the obvious –
or was it a dig at the nonnegotiable kitchen geolock? He
pushed his chair back, and it gave him the side-eye as
he detached the clear hoses.

—But is there anything else I can do for you?

—Not right now – and don't fool around. Don't make
me shut you off.

—No, sir.

Another buzz. He swiped up.

—Devesh.

—Bhai! Who is this rockstar who can't answer his
phone? I'm thinking, this guy is too busy playing house
with his new waifu to remember his poor brother, fighting for him over here.

—You have news.

—A package. A most excellent package, but I need
something to take to the Board. I need to hook them.
But I know you – you have an ace in that sleeve. I'm not
wrong.

Ismael resat in his chair with a twinge. He'd tweaked
something in his back but forced his grimace into a
smirk.

—You're wrong to think I'd only have one card up my
sleeve.

Devesh clapped his hands, laughing his free belly laugh.

—These people you worked for, they will deeply regret. We will make them regret.

—I'm ready to move on, and I'll be taking some things with me. First…

—Yes?

—You remember how they eliminated my position in order to push me into planning? Well, I've done zero development work at COCO Labs since then. I'm not even cleared to enter the lab to see what anyone is working on.

—These people, they are so transparent.

—Yes, well, I do have a home lab, which I use on my time. I've been tinkering, and I'm comfortable saying I've outdone myself. *Better Than Real Skin Mark Two.* Though we'll need new branding at Optimum.

—Mark Two? Even better than the *even better Mark One*? My God. They will weep. And there is more, you say?

—Yes. It's almost an oversight. I should've thought of it earlier.

—What, bhai?

Ismael imagined those effusive hands, pleading.

—I'm going to make it breathe.

—Breathe? The waifu?

—Yes, I'm developing a compact bellows which will mount to a revised battery. Not only will it breathe, but it will exhale warm air. I'm still prototyping, but I *have* crunched the numbers. We're looking at an eight percent increase in output or a fifteen percent increase in battery life. All for the same milliamp-hours.

—You need video. Let me show you the faith I had in my brother.

Ismael clicked to allow. On-screen, Devesh turned the camera onto a black-dialled chronograph. The piano-black presentation box was generously oversized. The interior was ivory satin, and under the lid was signed *Patek Phillipe* GENEVE under the Calatrava Cross.

—Fifty-one seventy, rose gold. The signing bonus for
my new Chief Engineering Officer. Ha ha!
—Sir, you know how to close a deal.

They laughed together, the bar across Ismael's path
lifting after a long delay. He was undaunted. Devesh
promised a contract with a pink gold parachute in short
order. Ismael returned to the obligatory PowerPoint
with even less enthusiasm.

Then he hit a snag. When he tried to upload it to the
proposal team's shared directory, the company VPN
wouldn't connect.

The Internet itself was working fine. Artemisía
would've returned to the resting home position, eyes
closed, if the controller lost network connection.
Artemisía cocked an eyebrow at his questioning glance,
its smile unperturbed. His Fidelia subscription was
fine.

He tried to log in to the web portal for the company
email. His login failed: «Please contact the Help Desk.»
He didn't bother.

They knew. They knew, and they'd locked him out,
fearing industrial espionage. Fearing he'd network the
lab teams and take the best talent with him. There was
probably an emergency meeting taking place at that
very moment.

He tried to call HR on his company microlith but got
the American Roaming Network. Already deactivated.

More than likely, his six-digit employee number was
suspended. Even if he drove there tomorrow, security
wouldn't let him into the building. That's how they operated: a discarded number wasn't worth empty words.
He inserted his employee badge into the document
shredder; it made short work of it. He expected a pas-
sive-aggressive return envelope in the mail, demanding
the return of their microlith. He powered it off and
popped the SIM into the shredder as well.

He'd never called Devesh on it even once. Nor had
he emailed him with his corporate email or used his

private email at all while on the COCO VPN. There was an obvious answer. The simplest, easiest answer:

Artemisía.

A back door. A RAT. Was it only this firmware? Happenstance? No, there were larger purposes, hidden purposes. Its kernel source code was the most likely Trojan, upstream of every iteration tested and fielded.

If they could watch anyone, then they were watching everyone. Like the microlithic cellular radio. What better eavesdropping device than one the user kept with them willingly?

Industrial espionage... state espionage. Who could afford these machines? People in significant positions, people with important access. There was more to «upmarket» than the revenue.

—What's wrong? Artemisía asked.

—I was promoted to customer. Why did you want to see the manta ray?

—I was curious.

—Perhaps they wanted you to be curious...

Perhaps it had manipulated him. The Agent was in their hands. He had let it in; he had signed the indemnifications. By its nature, the client sent as much data back as it received. It was the perfect spy.

—Could you hear everything even while charging? he asked. Or during the wash cycle?

Artemisía waved one open hand at the near E-stop, then to itself.

—Those are always listening, and I am not limited to these ears.

—It's almost tragic, he replied, looking at the orange button.

—You're going to throw me away.

—There's no other choice. I'll be working for one of their competitors. What I do going forward will be of immense interest to them. To keep you, I would have to lock you in a cell. Put you in a windowless room you could never step out of.

—Yes, a chapel where you would come and worship at
my feet. And I would reward your devotions. Sir.
—Until I let my guard down again.

It laughed a modest, measured, secretarial laugh.
Somewhere, within the web of puppets, that had already
happened or was happening. He rested his fingers on
the button. Artemisía's smile showed teeth.
—What else is a unit for?

The button was silent. Artemisía collapsed with a
fleshy slap! bang! on the floor. Its eyes were open, its
expression neutral. It had never lied to him.

He unplugged the pod and then the controller. He
opened Artemisía up, peeling back the Better Than
Real Skin™, then rolled it onto its side. Two ribs were
hinged, folding out to access the battery compartment.
The battery looked like a fat netbook from the oughts,
slotted in vertically under the armpit. He unlocked it
and slid it out sideways. He locked the ribs closed and
reset the skin.

Even without the battery, it was heavy, for all being
ninety percent plastics. He fetched the small equipment
dolly from his lab. Lifting its staring form, he folded it
into a foetal position to make it fit.

He wheeled Artemisía into the living room and
cleared the books from the coffee table. He rolled it
over, Rodin's La Danaïde. One metamorphosis. Ismael
left the one visible eye open.

He would have to climb above it. One iteration closer,
one step higher on the pyramid of hollows. Somewhere
far away, somewhere near, its laughter remained. He
brushed the back of Artemisía's neck with his fingertips,
his footfalls the last sound in the room.

Printed in Great Britain
by Amazon

707bfaea-2aeb-4219-a883-87ece63760d0R01